SURP

Slowly they adv
lying beside the fire, their weapons
the blanketed form. Suddenly, the desert night was shattered by the explosion of gunfire as the bandits emptied their weapons at their defenseless prey. The blanket jerked and snapped from the impact of bullets. As the smoke cleared, the leader kicked the blanket aside—revealing a pile of branches and grass shaped in human form. The bandits immediately cast nervous and panicked glances around the firelit grove. Then they heard the distinct sound of gun hammers being cocked.

"Up here," a voice snarled.

Jerking their gaze upwards, they saw a buckskin-clad man braced twenty feet above them in a cottonwood tree. In one hand was a Colt pistol. In the other, a rifle. And before they could even raise their guns, the Trailsman rained fire from above. . . .

COMANCHE BATTLE CRY

by

Jon Sharpe

A SIGNET BOOK

SIGNET
Published by New American Library, a division of
Penguin Putnam Inc., 375 Hudson Street,
New York, New York 10014, U.S.A.
Penguin Books Ltd, 27 Wrights Lane,
London W8 5TZ, England
Penguin Books Australia Ltd, Ringwood,
Victoria, Australia
Penguin Books Canada Ltd, 10 Alcorn Avenue,
Toronto, Ontario, Canada M4V 3B2
Penguin Books (N.Z.) Ltd, 182–190 Wairau Road,
Auckland 10, New Zealand

Penguin Books Ltd, Registered Offices:
Harmondsworth, Middlesex, England

First published by Signet, an imprint of New American Library,
a division of Penguin Putnam Inc.

First Printing, September 2001
10 9 8 7 6 5 4 3 2 1

The first chapter of this title originally appeared in *Cherokee Justice*,
the two hundred thirty-eighth volume in this series.

Printed in the United States of America

PUBLISHER'S NOTE
This is a work of fiction. Names, characters, places, and incidents either are the product of the author's imagination or are used fictitiously, and any resemblance to actual persons, living or dead, business establishments, events, or locales is entirely coincidental.

The Trailsman

Beginnings . . . they bend the tree and they mark the man. Skye Fargo was born when he was eighteen. Terror was his midwife, vengeance his first cry. Killing spawned Skye Fargo, ruthless, cold-blooded murder. Out of the acrid smoke of gunpowder still hanging in the air, he rose, cried out a promise never forgotten.

The Trailsman they began to call him all across the West: searcher, scout, hunter, the man who could see where others only looked, his skills for hire but not his soul, the man who lived each day to the fullest, yet trailed each tomorrow. Skye Fargo, the Trailsman, the seeker who could take the wildness of a land and the wanting of a woman and make them his own.

South of the Mexican Border, 1858—The trail to wealth and salvation follows the Rio Grande, but its riverbanks spill over with blood. Staying alive is like swimming upriver . . . if the tide doesn't drag you down, the current will. . . .

1

Skye Fargo had the unshakable sensation he was being followed.

The vague and elusive feeling that someone was trailing him caused a prickling along Fargo's backbone. Perhaps, he thought, it was some sixth sense warning him of approaching danger, but after a lifetime of living in the wilderness and surviving by his wits, determination, and sometimes luck, Fargo had learned to take his hunches seriously.

Every mile or two, Fargo reined up his Ovaro and scanned the dusty road behind him. The desert stretched for miles in every direction, rolling dunes dominating an arid landscape. In the distance, the seven-thousand-foot-high ridge of Texas's Chinati Mountains loomed purple. The only sound was the continual hiss of grains of sand being pushed along the desert floor by incessant wind.

In the distance, objects were distorted by heat shimmering up from the burning sands. Fargo removed his felt hat, wiped sweat from his forehead, and ran a hand through his matted hair.

Unable to shake the gnawing sense that he was being watched, Fargo checked the knotted rope attached to his packhorse, then turned his pinto back north, and continued on his journey.

* * *

Skye Fargo's trip to the Mexican state of Chihuahua had been long, hot, and tiring, but it would ultimately prove to be profitable. Anxious to obtain a herd of stout Mexican ponies to sell in Colorado, Fargo finally located a broker who put him in touch with a rancher who sold him forty-five head of the feisty *caballos* and made arrangements for the animals to be delivered within three months.

As Fargo returned across the arid Trans-Pecos region of West Texas, he longed for the high coolness of Colorado, accompanied by the scent of pine and spruce trees that grew thick in the foothills and mountain slopes.

The Colorado mountains were still six hundred miles away, however, and over half that distance would cover much more desert like the one he now rode across.

Another hour passed, and Fargo guided his horses to the brow of a low hill some fifty yards off the road. From the top of the prominence, he scanned his back trail once again, trying hard to make sense of flickering and shimmering shapes in the distance.

For one brief instant Fargo thought he saw something—the quick movement of a man or animal that didn't seem to fit in with the rest of the environment. Blinking sweat out of his eyes, he peered intently at the landscape behind him, but whatever it was had disappeared.

As the reddening sun nudged closer to the western horizon, Skye spotted a grove of cottonwood trees in the distance. One of the first lessons he had learned about the desert was that cottonwoods often meant water nearby, and he and his horses had not had a drink for over five hours.

Twenty minutes later, Skye guided his horses into the shaded relief of the grove. Near the middle of the cluster of thick trees, a small spring issued a clear stream of water that gurgled over the gravel of a narrow bed as it made its way down a gentle slope

Dismounting, Skye loosened his saddle cinch and led the Ovaro and Paco, his packhorse, to the stream. While the animals drank, he slapped the dust from his buckskin pants and examined the grove.

"Not a very defensible location," he said aloud, still unable to get rid of the feeling that he was being followed.

Laying a reassuring hand on the flank of his horse, he spoke softly to the stallion. "As bad as it is, this grove will be better than camping out in the open, and there's decent grass growing in a low spot over yonder for you and Paco."

After drinking from the cool spring, Skye removed the saddle and bridle from his pinto and the packs from Paco. Hobbling the two horses, he let them wander over to a low grassy area to graze. Skye knew mountain lions were common in this part of Texas, and he didn't want his animals to wander too far.

Within minutes, he'd gathered several armloads of cottonwood branches and had a small fire going. As bacon sizzled in his old cast-iron skillet, he rolled out a blanket, removed his boots, and leaned back against the bole of the largest tree. It was the first rest he had allowed himself in over twelve hours.

Skye's Colt remained belted on his hip. In one boot, a .32-caliber, two-shot derringer rested snugly in a specially made holster, and in the other he concealed his razor sharp Arkansas toothpick.

By the time the bacon was ready, twilight provided a setting for the calls and songs of desert frogs and insects as well as a number of night birds. Skye ate bacon and sopped the grease with a two-day-old biscuit he found in his pack.

In the light of a dying fire, he examined the loads in his revolver as he listened for sounds from the horses. The occasional swish of a tail, the stamp of a hoof, and the munching of grass in the distance provided an arrhythmic backbeat to the chorus of insects and frogs. The waxing moon provided a soft illumination to the grove.

As Skye replaced his revolver in a holster, all of the night sounds suddenly ceased, and a heart-stopping silence reigned in the grove.

Listening intently, Fargo thought he heard some new sounds coming from the south along the trail—the click of a horse's hoof against a rock, a barely audible jangle of harness. And then, carried through the night on the clear desert air, Fargo heard the whispers of men.

Strangers were coming to the spring.

About fifty yards from the grove of cottonwood trees, the burly leader in a black high-crowned hat signaled four riders to stop. With a grace belying his bulk, he slipped from the saddle, ground-hitched his mare, and pointed to the glow of the dying campfire in the distance.

"Leave your horses here," Frank Ormsby whispered to his companions. "We go the rest of the way on foot."

The four divided into pairs and fanned out on either side of their leader as they crept slowly toward the cottonwood grove. With the exception of Ormsby, who sported a trim moustache and a frock coat, the band of men were a ragged-looking lot, filthy from living along the desert trails and seldom encountering bathwater. Disheveled and dirty from spending months at a time far from civilization, these merciless road predators survived by murdering defenseless travelers and taking their money and belongings.

To the left of Ormsby a half-breed, the vile spawn of a cannibalistic Karankawa mother and a notorious Mexican outlaw, carried only a crude bow and three arrows. He moved so silently across the gravelly desert floor it seemed his feet never touched the ground.

Nearest to the half-breed was a man called "The Greek." Resting his hands on his holstered revolvers as he stalked toward the grove, The Greek gazed fixedly at the campfire and the sleeping form beside it. From time to time he ran his fingers down his long moustache hanging well below his dirty chin. Just one year earlier, The Greek was forced to flee from the city of New Orleans for killing three prostitutes. Once a pirate along the Atlantic coast, The Greek was no stranger to murder.

To the right of the leader was tall, lanky Jerome Cartwright, pistols at the ready in each hand. Angular in stature and jerky in his movements, Cartwright was wanted in Missouri for killing his father, mother, and three brothers.

Next to Cartwright walked Tito Benavides, gold teeth gleaming in the moonlight and rifle cradled lovingly in the crook of one arm. It was rumored that

Benavides had killed thirty men, and witnesses claimed he always smiled as he gunned down an adversary. The Mexican was smiling already in anticipation.

Frank Ormsby was the oldest of the five and the mastermind of the motley group of road agents. Known by several aliases across seven western states, he was originally from Arkansas and made his living over the years as a gambler, bank robber, extortionist, and confidence man. Discovering that preying on lone travelers and small wagon trains was easier than any of his previous occupations, Ormsby, along with a succession of killers that he recruited, pocketed small fortunes as they terrorized the remote portions of well-traveled roads throughout West Texas.

As the five men arrived at the periphery of the cottonwood grove, the half-breed pointed to the lone figure lying on the ground opposite the campfire. Curled up in a blanket, the man appeared to be sleeping soundly.

At a silent signal from Ormsby the men advanced, all weapons pointed toward the blanketed form.

When they were only fifteen feet from the reclining figure, Ormsby aimed his revolver and fired into the blanket. Instantly, the desert night was shattered by the explosion of gunfire as the bandits emptied their weapons at their defenseless prey. The blanket jerked and snapped from the impact of bullets.

Seconds later, as gun smoke and the pungent odor of gunpowder drifted from the grove, all was silent. Smiling, Ormsby picked up a stick of firewood, poked one end under the blanket, and flipped the cover aside.

Astonished, the five men looked down on a pile of branches and grasses arranged in such as way as to mimic human form. Realizing their error, the bandits immediately cast nervous and panicked glances about the moonlit grove.

"Up here," a voice snarled.

Jerking their gaze toward the sound, the predators spotted a man braced about twenty feet above them in the crotch of a thick cottonwood tree. In one hand was a Colt pistol. In the other, a rifle butt was propped against his thigh.

Skye pulled the triggers of both weapons simultaneously, the resultant explosion sounding like one shot. The Greek's eyes widened in surprise as blood poured from a hole that suddenly opened in the middle of his forehead. He fell backward to the ground only an instant before Cartwright, whose reedlike body jerked spasmodically in response to the bullet that tore through a chest artery.

As Ormsby and the half-breed dove for cover behind trees, Benavides was clumsily jamming shells into his rifle.

"Don't waste your time," Skye called down to the bandit. "You're already dead."

The Mexican looked up into the tree with an open-mouthed stare. Taking aim at the moonlight glittering from the gold teeth, Skye sent a bullet into the maw of his would-be killer. The bullet, traveling downward at an angle, struck Benavides, shattered several teeth and continued through bones of the neck, destroying nerves and muscle. Before Benavides crashed to the ground in death, his head flopped grotesquely forward onto his chest.

Positioning himself behind the protection of the cottonwood's trunk, Skye listened for the two remaining attackers. The sudden twang of a bowstring was followed by the thunk of an arrow into the tree only inches from his head.

A split second later, Skye heard someone running across the dried cottonwood leaves that littered the grove. Aiming at the noise, he alternately fired both guns in rapid succession until they were empty, and was rewarded by the sound of a falling body. In the moonlight, Skye saw the quivering form of the dying half-breed, his blood shining in dim light as it spread over the ground.

That leaves one more: the man in the big hat.

Deep silence greeted Fargo as he listened intently for some sound of the large man. He hesitated to climb down from the protection of the tree, fearing he might become an easy target. On the other hand, he didn't relish spending the night wedged among the branches.

As he considered his options, Fargo heard the sound of horses galloping away in the distance.

"So," Fargo mused aloud. "The big one chose to run away when he discovered the pickings weren't going to be so easy. And he's apparently taking the dead men's horses with him."

Climbing down the tree, Fargo listened to the fading sound of the retreating horses. As he reloaded his Colt, he peered in the direction of the fleeing attacker.

"Perhaps we'll meet again someday, big-hat," muttered Fargo, "and when we do I'll make certain you don't get the chance to prey on easy pickings again."

He put his mind on other things. When he got his mustangs to El Paso he would arrange to pasture them while he guided a man from New Orleans up the Rio

Grande by canoe, a job Fargo wouldn't have taken had the money not been so good. But scouting trails was also his business, and the upper Rio Grande was mostly unexplored territory, the land of the Mimbres Apache.

2

Fargo dipped his paddle into the smooth crimson water without taking his eyes from the shoreline. He was sure he saw movement somewhere in a stand of slender oak trees on a ridge to the north. Their bull-hide canoe swished through the Rio Grande's quiet waters like a knife through warm butter, despite its wide beam. Josh Brooks sat in the prow, muscular arms paddling easily as if he experienced no fatigue from previous days of travel against strong, steady currents northwest of El Paso. His sable skin bore a sheen of sweat, catching the late sunlight and giving the tall Creole fur trapper an aura not unlike the dark, oiled barrel of the Whitney rifle lying near his feet.

"I'd nearly swear I saw something up yonder," Fargo said.

"This sun can play tricks on a man's eyes," Josh warned as he studied the same wooded ridge. "I ain't seen nothin' move. Maybe it's the light."

It was true, the way a setting sun sometimes brought changes to even the most familiar shapes. It had been a dry fall and the gauzy sun dropped toward the earth through a haze of dust on the horizon. Colored light splashed on bare ground, painting an occasional tree trunk with ocher hues and turning fall oak and cottonwood leaves into sizzling displays of bright reds and dazzling yellows as though they were ablaze. The beauty of a western sunset never ceased to enthrall Fargo, particularly in this land of flaming reds and softer pastels. Even the land itself was blood-colored, as they traveled farther north. Where the land turned red, they were warned to be on the lookout for natives. *Red land meant red men along this river*, Buckshot Sims, an old friend of Fargo's, used to say. Sims had traveled this river enough to be taken seriously, but then again, Skye Fargo was no stranger to the Rio Grande.

Fargo paddled slowly, examining the ridge. Once, he glanced down to the Colt revolver lying atop a bundle of traps, its frame mottled by time and weather. The pistol wasn't accurate for any distance, but at close range a properly charged .36-caliber ball made a hell of a hole. For long-distance shooting his Henry rifle could center a raven's eye on the wing.

He watched the trees backgrounded by the soft colors of the sky, glazed by gold from the sun with leaves of crimson, orange, burnt umber and lightly freckled browns. Blue shadows formed below leafy limbs that turned to slate where no sunlight penetrated, a soft gray spot here and there, where fading light created the illusion of movement. He couldn't be sure.

The gentle gurgle of Josh's paddle passing through the sluggish current distracted Fargo from a closer look at a shadow beneath a sinewy branch. Another movement flashed and a splash of blue color emerged as a jay flitted from limb to limb, stirring the stillness with the flutter of its snow-edged wings. An oak leaf twisted on a breath of wind and fell from a branch, dancing and trembling as it swirled toward the orange-red earth below.

"I'm seeing things, I reckon," he told Josh in a feathery voice tinged with relief. They weren't looking for a confrontation with Indians. In one of the packs they had glass trading beads, cheaply made iron knives and some colorful ribbon, items Fargo liked to carry just in case he needed to play diplomat. Many Indians like bright colors and most had need for iron weapons.

"Maybe," Josh remarked softly, squinting in the sun's hard glare, crow's-feet webbing around his heavy-lidded eyes while he let his gaze wander upstream. Josh knew the fur business, but he didn't seem to know much about Plains Indian tribes.

The burble of water forking around the canoe's prow had a voice all its own, and there were times when Fargo didn't even hear it, having grown accustomed to its gentle music after paddling for so long. For almost two weeks they had moved steadily with the sun at their backs each morning. A grizzled boatman poling a raft of logs in the opposite direction told them five days ago that they'd seen the last of civilization at Bell's Hill, a small settlement on the southern bank where Texas-bound travelers bought supplies for the journey into the new republic. Fargo and Josh had heard stories of the war there, of a continuing fight with Mexico that promised to be long and full of hardships.

Again, he saw something move in the forest but this time it was not a bird . . . he was certain of it. "There," he said, pointing to a cluster of oak atop a knob where a feeder stream entered the river. "Look yonder in those trees, Josh. It sure as hell looked like somebody's hidin' in those oaks."

Sunlight streamed through a profusion of tree trunks and branches where Fargo was pointing, making it difficult to separate real objects from shadows. Light played off the smooth glaze that covered the oak and cottonwood leaves, making them sparkle like the flickering lights found in sapphires and diamonds, almost blinding with brilliance when leaves turned on breaths of gentle breezes.

"I don't see a damn thing 'cept trees, Skye."

"Maybe it was nothing."

Josh's paddle dipped into dark water, making ripples across the glassy surface. Cattails along the bank bent slightly when a whisper of air moved among them. Fargo watched the oaks steadily, unwilling to entirely dismiss what he'd seen, even though he had no idea what it was.

"Time we started lookin' for a place to camp," Fargo said, turning his broad face toward the south bank.

"Maybe we oughta look on that side, seein' as you're so sure there's somethin' on this side to worry 'bout," Josh replied smartly.

"I ain't worried. Bein' careful, is all. It'll be plumb dark in another hour. I'll fry up some catfish for supper."

"I'm gettin' tired of fish. Truth is, I've been sick of the taste of fish for years. If I never saw another fish in my whole life, it'd suit the hell outa me."

"That's what too many years on the river does to you." Fargo had learned that Josh had made most of his money running goods safely up and down the Mississippi, avoiding the pirates that terrorized other flatboat captains. "I can boil up some beans, only it's a shame to waste all this catfish meat."

After a sweep of his paddle, Josh lifted a piece of thick line from the water to inspect a squirming yellow catfish trailing along beside the canoe on cord threaded through the catfish's gills. "I guess you're right, Fargo. It'd be a shame if we had to feed him to the turtles, or one of them ol' coons. Biggest coons I ever saw in my life was livin' along the Mississippi. Weighed maybe forty pounds . . ."

Fargo was only half listening. Something had moved again high on the ridge. He shaded his eyes with a freckled hand. One tree in particular seemed highlighted by the sun's radiance as though it ignited like phosphor, a huge leafy torch standing alone among others in the forest. Behind the dark outline of its trunk, stood what looked like a silhouette of a man.

"See that biggest tree yonder," he said, pointing again to the ridge. "There's a man standin' behind it. I'd nearly swear an oath it's somebody watchin' us."

Josh returned the fish to the river. He stared at the ridge for a time. "I see it now," he said, speaking so softly that Fargo had trouble hearing him. "I reckon it could be a man."

Fargo knew sign language well—it was the easiest way to declare yourself as friendly. He rested his paddle across his lap and gave the sign for peace. Their canoe slowed against the current. He judged the distance at three hundred yards to the tree, maybe less. He signed again when nothing moved.

"Maybe it's only a tree," Josh suggested. "Hard to tell in this light." He picked up his paddle and continued rowing with slow, deliberate strokes.

"It's an Indian," Fargo said. "He's standin' real still so we can't be sure. I figure he's a lookout. He'll go back and tell the others about us. We could have visitors tonight."

Josh wasn't quite ready to agree yet. Paddling steadily, he kept glancing to the ridge between strokes. "Didn't you say we'd know if they was Osages by their shaved heads? That Apaches have long hair braided in a single strand down their backs, and Comanches got two braids, only they'll be farther upriver?"

Fargo recalled almost every detail he knew about traveling this river. Back when Josh contacted him about running the Grande, Fargo's stomach turned. For the man they called Trailsman and a seasoned flatboat pilot with experience battling gangs of river thieves and the most brutal weather imaginable in winter, this trek should have held few real challenges, but Fargo knew better. For whatever reason the Rio Grande always brought Fargo bad luck, and if the money hadn't been as good as it was, he would have told Josh to shove it! "Whatever breed he is, he ain't movin' at all, just standin' there behind that tree like he was a part of it." He resumed paddling in concert with Josh as the canoe came abreast of the ridge, gliding silently toward a setting ball of orange-red sun hovering above the river, flaming over the landscape. Changing the angle from which he watched the tree made no visible change in the silhouette beside it.

"Leastways he ain't shootin' arrows at us," Josh said under his breath, "if it is an Injun."

"I suppose we oughta be grateful for that," Fargo agreed, as they slipped past the ridge unmolested. When he looked up at the tree again, the silhouette was gone. Now he was certain it had been someone watching them. "He's gone, Josh. Unless he went to water the cactuses, I think we're about to have some company."

Josh's head turned quickly to the north as soon as the words left his mouth. He stiffened, halting the motion of his paddle abruptly. "Look yonder, Skye," he said, suddenly sounding grave. "You was right, there's five of 'em. They's ridin' scrawny little ponies . . ."

As the canoe drifted past a deep ravine leading down to the river, Fargo saw what Josh had seen. Five bronze-skinned men on small, multicolored horses watched the canoe from a canebrake at the bottom of the wash. Two carried lances with feathers tied to painted shafts. The others had bows slung over their shoulders or resting across the withers of their ponies.

"Sweet Jesus," Josh whispered, his heart pounding. He sat there, frozen like he was trapped in a block of ice for several seconds, holding his breath until he heard Fargo speak.

"I'm gonna give 'em the sign for peace," Fargo said calmly.

He opened his palm and held it forward, fingers together with his thumb extended. The Indians seemed to ignore him, sitting passively on the backs of their ponies as he continued to give the sign. Straight rays of sunlight made them appear as red as the river, somewhat copper-colored even, after a closer examination.

"Either they don't know what it means, or they just don't care," he said, as they drifted slowly past the mouth of the ravine in full view of the Indians. He continued to hold his hand in the same manner. Stalks of cane teetered in a current of air around the riders, swaying gently behind five lean, bare-chested men. Fargo had lived and hunted among most of the tribes that were scattered across the land. He had fought with them and for them, had killed their sons and loved their daughters. As a people they had earned his respect. The Cherokee, the Navajo, the Flathead, the Sioux, the Kiowa and the Arapaho were as much a part of the land he loved as the coyote and the deer. Fargo respected them as much as he did any other people who followed the trail. While he admired their culture and feared their wrath, he felt he understood why they inspired so many tales of terror. These men were quite clearly part of a far more hostile race than the Cherokee or Seminole. He had the feeling he was seeing something truly dangerous, like a pack of wolves.

They stared at him and he stared back. It was only a feeling, a vague uneasiness he felt when they looked at him, but he was certain they viewed him and Josh as prey.

"They ain't Osages," Josh said again, sitting motionless as the canoe continued to glide past the ravine. "They's got a whole headful of hair . . . black as crow feathers."

Current tugged at the canoe, slowing it to a crawl. Fargo lowered his hand and whispered, "Keep paddlin'. They don't act like they'll harm us. If we keep paddlin' maybe they'll see we don't mean them harm." He gripped his paddle in two gnarled fists and forced the blade to take a deep bite out of the river.

One Indian on a blue roan pony turned his head and spoke to the others, making some sort of gesture with his hand just as the canoe carried them out of sight. Fargo's mouth felt dry and cottony, as they continued westward toward a glowing sunset, watching the riverbank for evidence that they were being followed. Now light and shadow became so intermingled in trees lining the river that he found it impossible to distinguish shapes or movement. With his heart hammering he paddled harder while guiding the canoe farther from the east bank, just in case the air filled with speeding arrows or feathered lances. Josh's powerful strokes helped carry them quickly toward the middle of the broad river.

A blazing sun dipped toward the distant Pacific Ocean half a continent beyond them, dropping below a hilly horizon lined with trees where a watery highway stretched endlessly to touch a fiery sky. Fargo worried about the colors, so many reds, like a veil of blood over the land.

But if things went as Fargo planned, he'd be heading back down the river to El Paso in a couple of weeks to collect his mustang ponies with two hundred dollars in gold for his trouble. Then he could head on over to Colorado to make his sale. All he had to do was find beaver country for Josh Brooks and climb back in this empty canoe, traveling with the current, hardly paddling at all . . .

3

Crickets chirped from tall grasses near the fire. Fireflies danced in the black forests around them, winking just beyond a circle of light from crackling flames. A drooping willow near the water cast a dark shadow over the river where their canoe was tied to a low limb. Fargo sat with his back to the trees, gazing north across the river, while Josh turned pieces of frying catfish in a cast-iron skillet.

"They'll see our fire," Josh said. "They'll know we're here."

Josh's face appeared more deeply etched by angry lines with the fire below him. He was past forty, almost bald, yet still as fit as any man Fargo had ever known. He stood six and a half feet tall in boots and possessed incredible strength. His mother had been Creole, he said, speaking French and a few words of broken English. His father was a slave brought over from Africa. Both his parents died during a cholera outbreak in New Orleans. He was eleven years old, homeless and starving when he went to work on a flatboat poling the Mississippi.

"They already know we're here, Josh. They seen us plain as day," Fargo said.

He'd been edgy ever since. Perhaps it was their first

look at an unfamiliar tribe that was so unsettling. "They didn't act like they were all that glad to see us," he muttered, staring across silver water, eyes roaming up and down the bank like he expected to see more of them in the dark.

"Maybe they never saw a freed man before. Leastways they wasn't shootin' no arrows at us. Thank the Almighty for small things. We ain't dead yet . . ." He turned a catfish strip and frowned when he saw how black it was. "This fish is ready."

"I'm not all that hungry. Eat what you want an' I'll eat some later."

Josh grinned a little. "You got a bad case of the nerves, Fargo? Can't be no worse'n river pirates," Josh said, bringing a strip of catfish steak to his mouth on the tip of his knife, testing it for heat with his tongue. He chewed thoughtfully a moment. "I remember a bunch that jumped me and my crew south of Tiptonville. Those boys hailed from Kentucky. They was all kin, three brothers an' the rest was cousins. Jumped us from an island we didn't even know was there. I still got scars from that one, where that ball like to have took off my leg. Indians can't be no worse'n them. They was damn sure plenty hard to kill . . . like a wild pig that's wounded, chargin' straight at us like they wasn't afraid of dyin'.

Skye Fargo had been on more sides of more battles than he could remember. If it were up to him he'd rather not add to that list. "If we can, we're gonna deal with these Indians peacefully," he said, watching the river. "You may think you're gonna get rich bringin' furs to New Orleans next spring, but the only way they'll let you trap in this country is if we convince them we're peaceful. Offer 'em whatever we can for the right to stay here and get you settled."

Josh ate more fish. "The part 'bout gettin' rich sounds real good. I've been poor so long I ain't sure I'll know how to act."

"Stayin' alive long enough to sell your furs will be your best start. If you find as much beaver as I heard was here, it won't be long till you've got yourself a nice little business. Three or four winters, maybe five. And if you get lucky, you can live like a king for the rest of your days. Beaver pelts are bringin' a half dollar down there."

Josh seemed to be contemplating something. "When more folks hear 'bout all this fur-trappin' country, they'll be comin' too, like me. If I was to open a tradin' post up river a ways, I could sell 'em supplies. Maybe even buy their furs at a fair price an' boat 'em down to New Orleans myself. Flatboats can work this river, what I've seen of it. I could get me some flatboats an' hire honest crews."

"I've been thinkin' the same thing. Only problem's gonna be those Indians. I can't figure how we'll explain what we aim to do." Fargo listened to the river. "All they did was watch us like we wasn't supposed to be here."

"You worry too much, Skye." Josh glanced around them at the trees, nibbling fish from his knifetip. "If they wanted to stop us they'd have attacked. All they done was sit there, watchin' us float by like we was driftwood. Time to worry is when they start shootin' at us. Till then I'm gonna rest easy. You could see they ain't got any rifles. If it's a fight they're after, we'll oblige 'em."

Fargo wasn't so sure. Remembering the way they

looked, he wasn't sure obligin' them was the best idea. "I reckon we'll know in a few days if they'll let us pass. We'll find most of the beaver dams, up that river comin' from those mountains way to the north. They're called Wichitas, after a local tribe."

Josh stirred around in the skillet with his knife until he found the right piece of fish. An owl hooted across the river as he spoke.

Somewhere to the south a screech tore through the night. When Fargo turned he found Josh was looking, too. They both recognized the cry of a nighthawk.

"Likely only huntin' rabbits," Josh remarked, casting a look at the sky. "They scream like that when they're huntin', sometimes."

Fargo watched the river again, patiently listening to the night. He glanced over his shoulder and saw Josh staring into the darkness as well. Josh leaned forward as though he'd heard or seen something out of place. "What is it?" he asked.

"Can't say for sure," Josh replied, lowering his voice. He reached for his rifle, resting it on his knees. "Could be you've got me jumpy. Somethin' moved out there just now. Maybe it's only a wild pig feedin' at night. I thought I heard somethin'."

Fargo grabbed his Henry, checking the percussion cap with his thumb. "Which direction? Point to it."

Josh aimed his knife. "Yonder, I think. Couldn't be sure of it. Only heard it once . . ."

They sat in silence, craning their necks to listen to forest sounds.

"Crickets stopped chirpin'," Fargo said, suddenly aware of how quiet it was. A bullfrog was singing somewhere upriver.

"Somethin' out there disturbed 'em," Josh replied, coming to a low crouch with his rifle. He took his pistol from one of the packs, hunkering down as he crept away from the firelight toward a tree trunk. "I can't see a damn thing movin' out there besides fireflies," he whispered, moving over to the tree on the balls of his feet. "Maybe we oughta douse those flames . . ."

"Too late for that," Fargo answered softly from a nearby tree trunk, peering south into the night. "They already seen it, if we've got company. They'll come if they want, best we can do is be ready."

Fargo listened. Behind him, the river burbled quietly as the current drifted by their camp. Off in the distance the same bullfrog croaked endlessly, sounding like a huge fireplace bellows with a hole in it.

They remained hidden in the forest for several minutes. Josh began to sweat until his hands felt clammy around his rifle stock, while tiny beads of perspiration formed on his face and neck and arms. The silence lingered, deepening when the bullfrog suddenly stopped croaking upstream. "I can't see anything," he whispered. Their fire cast wavering shadows among the trees, creating the illusion of movement.

Fargo blinked when he thought he saw a large shape between two trees. "There. Look right there between those big oaks to your left. It looked just like a horse. I'd nearly swear I saw a horse walk between 'em."

Josh examined the trees carefully. "You're seein' things, Skye. Ain't no horse over yonder. Besides, we'd have heard it if it was somethin' big as a . . ." He stopped abruptly when a shadow stirred, taking shape before their eyes. Then more shadows began moving to the left and right, inky forms advancing closer to the firelight.

"Indians," Josh gasped, keeping his voice low. "They're all around us." He swung his rifle to his shoulder and thumbed back the hammer. His hands were trembling.

"Don't shoot," Fargo warned. "Maybe they didn't come after our hair. Let's see what they want before we start shootin' at 'em. Could be they're friendly." Fargo focused on a bare-chested Indian man on the back of a willowy pony. "It's them," he told Josh gravely, "the same ones we saw before. They must have crossed the river to get at us, only there's a hell of a lot more of 'em this time." He counted more than a dozen Indians in forest shadows around the fire.

When the Indians were a little more than fifty yards away they stopped almost in unison, as though there was some prearranged distance they meant to keep. They had bows, and some held feathered spears like the ones they saw at the river before dark.

Fargo lowered his rifle, wondering if showing himself might be a mistake. He stood up slowly and held out one hand, making the sign for peace.

Not one Indian moved or returned the sign. They sat on their ponies quietly, staring at Josh and Fargo. Fargo kept his palm open, waiting for some show of recognition. "They don't understand it at all. All they're doin' is starin' at me."

Before Fargo could decide what to do next, an Indian wheeled his pony and rode back into the forest shadows. The others turned and disappeared as silently as they had come.

When the last Indian was out of sight, Fargo lowered his palm and let out the breath he was holding.

"Wonder what that was all about?" he asked Josh, bewildered by their sudden departure.

"Maybe they was just testin' us," Josh replied, sounding as relieved as Fargo felt when they found themselves alone again.

4

Josh was still shaken long after the Indians departed and he'd been unable to sleep. As dawn came he allowed himself to relax somewhat, although he still found himself examining the forest closely, half expecting to see the early morning skies fill with a swarm of speeding arrows.

Fargo crawled out of his bedroll at first light, stretching and yawning before he took the coffeepot to fill it at the river. He gave Josh a sideways glance. "You don't look so good this mornin'."

"I couldn't sleep. Didn't appear those Indians bothered you any."

He sauntered back to the fire and put a handful of coffee beans in the pot before nestling it in a bed of glowing coals. "I kept an eye open, but if they wanted to scalp us they'd have tried it. They showed themselves instead. All in all, they acted peaceful as any man could ask for. You're headed for an early grave with all that worryin'." Skye watched the sun rise slowly, not yet visible above the horizon. "It's hard to figure why they came though. They let us get a good look at them, but that's all. No sense to it. Why didn't they try to find out what we're up to? Why we're here?"

"Maybe they guessed we was trappers and that's why they let us be. Maybe they was only curious 'bout us, seein' what we looked like up close."

"They had their faces painted. That means they're lookin' for a fight."

"I've heard it said before 'bout Injuns. This bunch didn't act like they wanted a war with us. They just rode off mindin' their own business."

"Sure don't make any sense to me that all they wanted was to get a look at us." Fargo walked down to the river and knelt to splash water on his face, paying only scant notice to his reflection on the surface. A tangled mane of dark hair fell below his shoulders and his beard needed a trim. He'd lost so much weight since they started up the river his buckskin pants fit too loosely, requiring another notch in his belt. He thought of himself as fit—he had to be to survive the life he led. Years riding the wilderness hardened his muscles to iron. When he saw dark circles under his eyes he shook his head and chuckled. Maybe he should listen to his own advice and stop worrying himself into an early grave over a few Indians just because they were a breed he'd never dealt with before.

He rinsed out his mouth and washed his face, gazing across the river absently. It would be a while before he forgot about their visitors last night, how close they came. Fargo had picked up their movement long before they came, but there was still no stopping them. They looked like wild creatures up close, with slashes of white paint on their cheeks.

Fargo inspected their canoe carefully before wandering back to the fire, smelling coffee, wishing he had his Ovaro for the rest of their journey. "Let's hit the river early," he said, squatting near the flames. "I'd just as soon put some distance behind us today." Scanning the forest, he couldn't quite shake the familiar feeling that they were being watched.

It was a most unexpected sight. A two-wheel cart drawn by a shaggy brown donkey was bogged in shallow water near the river's edge. A man dressed in priest's garb stood belly-deep in water, trying to free his stranded animal, pulling on its bridle for all he was worth. A noonday sun shone down on the priest's floundering efforts as Fargo and Josh paddled around a bend in the river.

"Can't believe my own two eyes," Josh exclaimed, swinging the prow toward the south bank where the donkey was bogged. "I never figured we'd see another soul up this river besides wild Injuns."

Fargo watched the robed cleric with the same amazement. "Hard to figure what he's doin' way out here. Why would a priest be so far from any kind of church?"

"Maybe he's lost. He's sure as hell stuck. That's liable to be quicksand, Skye." Josh hurried his paddle strokes, taking deeper bites out of the river.

Fargo quickened his paddling. Their canoe sliced through red water soundlessly, but it was the sight of movement that caught the priest's attention. He looked up from his efforts to dislodge the donkey and cart. For a moment he stood motionless in the river, staring at the canoe like he couldn't quite trust his eyes. He then began to wave frantically, yelling, "Over here, my friends! Over here!"

Fargo noted the priest's darker skin. "We're coming! Don't fight the sand! We'll pull you out!"

The canoe moved swiftly toward the bank. Now Fargo could see the priest's face clearly. He was Spanish or Mexican—not a surprise since this territory was still a part of Mexico—judging by his skin color, frail-looking, thin to the point of starvation. A bald spot on the top of his head shone brightly in light from the sun, although he appeared to be young, in his middle thirties or perhaps even younger.

They paddled closer to shore. Fargo noticed how the priest's arms were shaking with fatigue.

"My donkey is sinking deeper!" he cried. "He can't move and I can't lift his hooves!"

"We'll help you!" Josh shouted, aiming for an open spot near a willow tree shading the bank. "You're in quicksand. We've got ropes."

They reached land and stepped out in murky shallows. Fargo took a length of rope from one of the packs. "Just hold on until we get there, Father," he said, feeling sucking sand tug at his feet. Moving through quicksand required know-how, something any seasoned river boatman learned early if he meant to stay alive.

Josh reached the donkey cart first, as Fargo was coming with the rope.

"I'm so thankful," the priest said, smiling weakly, his face beaded with sweat and river water. "This is surely an act of God when the two of you came through this wilderness now. My donkey would have drowned . . . he can't free himself, and I am not strong enough to help him."

Fargo struggled over to the donkey's head, slipping a noose around its neck. He nodded at the priest. "We were surprised to find anyone else so far from civilization, Father. All we've seen so far are Indians."

He tossed the end of the rope over to Josh and said, "I'll lift its feet while you pull him around. I can tell he ain't buried all that deep."

Josh wound the rope around his waist and leaned against it as Fargo grabbed the donkey's right foreleg. They were near enough to shore that the water was not fully waist deep.

Josh's pulling freed the donkey almost at once. It made a lunge to free its rear legs as Josh swung the animal around to lead it from the river. The wooden cart made a cracking noise, wheels groaning in protest as it came out of the mud and sand. Josh led the donkey up the bank while Fargo and the priest pushed the cart from behind.

Once on dry land, the priest sleeved sweat from his brow and turned to them. "I'm so very, very grateful to you both. My name is Father Olivares." He offered his hand to Fargo, then to Josh. "I have been lost for weeks now, with almost nothing to eat and no map to guide me. I managed to snare a few rabbits to keep me alive. By the grace of God, you came along just when things were at their worst. I was trying to cross this river, hoping to find an outpost, some form of civilization. I was told there was a place called Bell's Hill along the river, a trading post. I've been traveling down this bank for days now and there has been no sign of habitation."

Fargo grinned. "You missed it by many miles, Father. It's east of here, maybe by a hundred miles or more. I'm Skye Fargo and this is Josh Brooks. We're headed upriver. We passed Bell's Hill five or six days ago."

"Dear God," Olivares whispered, leaning against the side of his cart for support, shaking his head. "It would appear I have no sense of direction. I used the sun as my guide. For days I went with nothing to eat and I grew so weak I was dizzy. I must have wandered off course." He took a deep breath, and there was sorrow in his voice when he spoke again. "Quite clearly, I'm not suited for this inhospitable land. I don't belong here. If you hadn't come along my donkey would have drowned. I was too weak to pull it out without your assistance."

"We'll fix you something to eat, Father," Fargo promised. "As soon as we get a fire goin' we'll cook some bacon and coffee. If you want, lie down and rest for a spell. You look like you're a little bit unsteady on your feet. I'll unharness your donkey for you while Josh gets the fire started. Then you can tell us what it was that brought you way out here."

The priest nodded his thanks, adjusting a piece of rope girding his robe around his stomach. "I'm in your debt, Mr. Fargo, yours and Mr. Brooks's. If you had not come along when you did I would be without my donkey. God has been merciful, sending you to me in my hour of need. I can help with the harness. The offer of food is greatly appreciated, kind sirs. As you must be able to tell I'm not adaptable to this wilderness. My superior, Father Tomas, gave me a map to Mission Santa Fe, where I was to help with our efforts to teach the Indians Christianity. I've gotten lost. My map says there is a trading post somewhere along the way."

Fargo began unfastening harness straps while the priest was talking. "Never heard of no mission named Santa Fe, Father, but there's a village farther north by that name. Wherever it is, it sure ain't so far south along this river. We didn't know about a trading post.

As to bein' where you can help teach religion to Indians, there's plenty of them around, only I wouldn't count on them bein' interested in learnin' about bein' a Christian. The ones we saw didn't look too interested. I'd hate to be the first man to try to preach to 'em." He peered through the cart's slatted sides, finding canvas packs and a large wooden crucifix almost four feet long wrapped in a piece of burlap.

"Santa Fe is a new mission to the Indians. Father Augustine and a party of workmen traveled there last fall to build a church. They sent a messenger to Mexico City asking for more supplies, describing the hardships. Father Tomas directed me and a young priest, Father Esteban, to bring what was needed to Santa Fe. We had our carts full of sugar and corn and a variety of seeds to prepare a garden, and two soldiers from the garrison to protect us. But quite unexpectedly, war was declared, and the two soldiers escorting us northward revolted, robbing me of my purse and all our supplies, leaving only a few sacred ornaments for the church. Father Esteban was killed. I felt I could not turn back. Alas, it would seem I should have done so. I have failed Father Augustine and his workers quite miserably. Even if I am able to find them, there is little left for his gardens. Most of my seeds were taken when they stole our food. I still have a few seeds, and some sugar, but what will it matter if I'm unable to locate Father Augustine and the mission? I'm utterly lost without my map. I must find that smaller village, the trading post."

"Sounds like you're lucky to be alive, Father Olivares."

Hearing this, Olivares looked askance and bowed his head as though in shame. "I'm afraid I ran away into the woods, leaving poor Father Esteban to his fate. I hid from them until they left with our supplies." He said it softly, keeping his face to the ground. "I was never a brave man. I vowed to give my life to the order, helping the poor, devoting my life to the church. If I had known Father Tomas meant to send me into a wilderness full of hostiles, I might have chosen otherwise. This experience has sorely tested my faith, I fear. My prayers have asked God to be patient with me."

Fargo lowered the donkey's shafts and led it over to a tree, tying it to a low limb. He watched Josh blowing gently on a few sparks in the tinder, begging flames to life. "We've got a real crude map of this river, if it'll help."

Olivares walked unsteadily to a tree trunk near Josh's fire and sat down against it, removing his muddy sandals. For a time he rested his head against the tree, breathing deeply. "It was to be built north of a place where two rivers joined. We were instructed to follow the smaller river to a mountain range where a tribe of nomads live. They call themselves Mimbres."

"Mimbres Apaches," Fargo said, squatting down to watch Josh add sticks to his fire, thinking out loud. "Sounds like we're headed to nearly the same place. Mr. Brooks intends to trap furs along the Rio Grande, which runs right through Apache country. There's a big creek that joins with this river, somewhere west of here, only we ain't exactly sure where it is ourselves. We know there's plenty of Apaches, an' we were told they can be mean as hell."

Olivares frowned a little. "Father Augustine wrote that he made peace with them. They left him alone. However, they did not appear to be interested in learning the word of God. It was his plan to win them over with gifts and kindness. With a garden and an orchard, gifts of fruit and vegetables would clearly show our friendliness. Sadly, I lost most of our seeds. I have very few left, some peach and pear seeds, and almost no vegetables. By Father Augustine's writings, these Mimbres are predominantly meat eaters. They worship things in nature, such as the moon and sun, the earth itself which they call Earth Mother. I spent months in preparation for this journey, learning some of their language, as much as I could from the journal Father Augustine sent to Father Tomas. Now, all is lost. I have failed Father Tomas miserably, and perhaps because of my failure, Father Augustine and his five young Franciscans will also fail. The robbers took everything, including the life of a dedicated priest."

"You learned some of their language?" Fargo asked, glancing over to Josh briefly.

"A few words and simple phrases, the ones Father Augustine sent to Mexico City in his journal of the mission's difficulties during the winter."

Fargo saw a plan unfolding, one that would help him and Josh establish relations with the Indians and hopefully keep them alive. "If we took you along with us to that creek we're lookin' for, you could explain to those Apaches what we wanted, that Mr. Brooks only wanted to trap furs in exchange for some trinkets we brought with us."

"I suppose we could travel together . . ." Olivares agreed thoughtfully.

Josh got up, looking west. "You could follow along in your cart until we get where we're going, Father. We've got food, and me an' Skye would enjoy the company. You should be able to go the rest of the way to

Santa Fe alone." He ambled down toward the river to get a frying pan and coffeepot without waiting for a reply.

The priest sat quietly for a moment, then he nodded. "It is clearly God's will that you found me, Mr. Fargo. Let us work together. I will speak for you with the Mimbres, and if you wish, I can teach you some of their language as well. I gladly accept your proposition. We shall travel together, wherever the will of the Lord takes us."

Fargo offered no opinion as to what forces would take them to good beaver country. Privately, he was convinced a keen eye and a steady hand on rifle stood the best chance of getting them where they wanted to go.

It was good news that an outpost of some kind lay ahead of them on the river, probably little more than a general store and a saloon or two. But it would keep the Apaches from making a move against them in that section of the river, a welcome thought after what they'd seen in the firelight.

5

Later that day, Fargo and Josh paddled their canoe to a small village. Olivares followed them along the banks of the river, which ran through a broad valley between the Van Horn Mountains on the east.

"Men with dreams," Fargo said to Josh. "Men who don't understand that easy money and hard times go hand in hand. Too many greenhorns to count, and too few of them stand a chance with the lack of water, raiding Indians, and other hardships. Damn fools."

Josh offered a snort in response.

"Sometimes I don't know whether to admire them for trying or scorn them for their arrogance." Fargo continued, paddling toward the west bank. There were four small buildings in the trading post, made from adobe bricks or thin, weathered planking. It was so new to the region it wasn't even on the map. Fargo didn't even think it had a name yet.

It was like many other towns in the Mexican desert, Fargo thought to himself. In the wake of growing numbers of travelers headed west, livelihood in this virtually unsettled wasteland was usually limited to staples, including whiskey, and a cool place to wash it down, usually provided by enterprising businessmen who arrived and opened mercantiles, hardware stores, and banks. A short time later, more saloons would appear, followed by a livery, a bordello, a piece goods store, and maybe even a church.

Towns like this, in the middle of the desert, seldom survived, Fargo thought. Located far from railroads and dependent on unreliable water wells and shallow rivers that could dry up any day, settlements like this one were doomed.

Fargo and Josh paddled up to the shore and got out. The priest and his donkey cart were not far behind them.

A plank building looked as if it had been hastily constructed, but it was clean and well cared for. In a corral behind the building, Fargo noticed a small pack of horses lolling near the crosspoles.

A stout, bearded, leather apron–clad man carrying blacksmith tongs emerged from the interior shadows and waved a greeting at the newcomers. Fargo returned the wave and walked up to the building.

"Saw you comin' in," said the owner with a cheerful ring in his voice. "Don't get many strangers out this way much. My name's Beeson."

"Skye Fargo," Fargo said as the two men shook hands. "My companions are Josh Brooks and Father Olivares. He'll need a place to stable his donkey for the night, and a spot where he can park his cart."

"Skye Fargo!" The liveryman's eyes widened in renewed appraisal of his visitor. "Would you be the Skye Fargo who cleaned out that pack of outlaws up in Colorado Territory a couple of years back?"

"Maybe."

"Mighty pleased to meet you, Mr. Fargo," Beeson said as he led the way back to his forge. "Folks drift in here from time to time with stories about shootists and their guns. It seems that every other one of 'em got a story 'bout the Trailsman. Until now, I always thought you was made up."

Wanting to change the subject, Fargo asked the liveryman if he could check the donkey's hooves, since the animal seemed to be limping on a foreleg.

Beeson increased the heat in the forge by pumping the old leather Winslow Brothers bellows with his right foot. Picking up a horseshoe with the tongs, he responded, "Sure can. I got clean stalls and a bit of corn for the donkey. It'll be ten cents a day to stable him."

The liveryman walked over just as Olivares arrived and lifted the donkey's gimpy leg and examined the hoof.

"He's got a split hoof, Mr. Fargo. This donkey ain't goin' to be able to travel much farther."

"You got a spare you can sell us?"

"Just so happens I do," said Beeson. "A big feller brought in a half-dozen horses for sale yesterday and I got 'em real cheap. They been rode hard and was in bad shape. Just needed some rest and feed was all. They're out back if you want to look them over."

Fargo's ears picked up. People sold and traded horses all the time, it was a way of life out here, but any man who took in six horses at once was either a regular trader or a thief. What caught Fargo's suspicion was that any trader worth his weight knew to freshen up his horses before selling them in order to get the best price. Curious, Fargo asked, "What did this man look like, the man who sold you the horses?"

"Kind of a big feller with a small moustache," said Beeson, "and he wore a big, black, high-crowned hat."

"Do you know where he is now?"

"Sure do. He's over at the saloon, playin' cards with some of the locals. Beatin' 'em badly at poker, they tell me."

"Thanks," Fargo said, as he began helping Olivares and Josh with the donkey's harness. "Pick out the best one of those six horses, one that's broke to wagon, and make me a good deal on it."

Beeson gave the donkey cart a critical eye. "If this here padre intends to follow the Rio Grande north, there's some real steep canyons. This wagon an' a horse won't make it unless he swings wide of the river by a mile or so."

"Mr. Fargo," Olivares whispered, "I do not have the money to pay for a new horse."

"I'll pay for it," Fargo said. "But I've got business to attend to first." Hanging the harness on a wooden peg, Fargo told Beeson, "I'll be down at the saloon. My friends will be waiting for me here. By the way, what's the name of this town?"

"Red Hawk. That's also the name of our saloon," Beeson said.

"I'll go with you," Josh said, carrying his Paterson in his belt.

"I can handle this alone. Stay here. Just make me the loan of your pistol, in case there's more than one of 'em."

Josh handed over his piece, and nodded silently as Fargo walked toward the saloon.

The dense smell of stale beer and cigar smoke instantly greeted Fargo as he pushed his way through the bat-wing doors and into the smokey interior of the Red Hawk Saloon.

Making toward the bar at the opposite end of the building, Fargo spotted what looked like the familiar shape of a man wearing a big hat and playing cards. Sunshine filtering through the dirty window nearby afforded the only light for the four gamblers seated at a table in the far left corner.

Only one or two of the drinkers and card players in the Red Hawk paid notice to Fargo's entry, and the piano player never missed a beat as the tall stranger strode across the hard dirt floor.

As Fargo neared the crude plank bar, the bartender greeted him with a friendly smile.

"Welcome, stranger," he said. "What'll it be for you?"

The bartender's dirty apron sagged around his thin frame. The hair of his thick, brushy moustache hung well over his upper lip. The pallor of his skin and the dimness of his eyes suggested to Fargo that the man seldom saw the sunshine.

"Whiskey," Fargo said. "I've got several days' worth of dust I need to wash out of my throat." As an afterthought, Fargo fixed the bartender's gaze and said, "I want the good stuff you keep under the bar, not that snake-head juice you serve the locals."

Smiling, the bartender reached beneath the bar and brought forth a bottle, uncorked it, and poured three fingers of a deep amber fluid into a clean glass. Leaning toward Fargo he said in a low tone, "Kentucky's finest. I save it for those few who know the difference."

Fargo smiled back his thanks and laid a coin on the bar.

"My name is Henry Fant," said the bartender, extending a bony hand.

"Skye Fargo." Fargo's huge work-toughened hand completely covered the bartender's.

Fant bent forward for a better look at the newcomer as he pondered the name. "Are you the Skye Fargo from up near the Rocky Mountains who is supposed to have killed a hundred men?"

"A hundred may be an exaggeration," Fargo replied, indifferent to the stories that followed him around. "Besides, I never killed anybody who didn't deserve it."

Fant beamed. "Skye Fargo. Well, I'll be, the Trailsman himself, right here in the Red Hawk Saloon!"

As Fant moved away to wait on another customer, Fargo relaxed against the heavy planks and regarded the men at the poker table.

The gambler wearing the big hat was burly and tall. Even seated, he was a full head taller than any of the other men playing cards. He had a large head, and waves of sandy brown hair streamed out from under his hat. A pair of large and bushy eyebrows appeared to connect above the bridge of the nose. The eyes were dark, a menacing blue, sunk deeply into the sockets.

Though he appeared to be carrying around some extra fat, he had an aura of power and confidence about him. Fargo thought he had the look of a man who would likely fare well in a fistfight, and undoubtedly had many times in the past. He had found the leader of the gang that tried to jump him below the border, of this Fargo was certain.

While he watched the table, the man in the big hat raked in one pile of winnings after another. Every now and then one of the other players would quit in disgust and leave, his place immediately taken by another. The stack of winnings at the gambler's right elbow looked like it might total nearly four hundred dollars.

As he observed the ongoing game, Fargo noticed the big man deftly palming cards and dealing others from the bottom of the deck.

"I can't stand a card cheat," muttered Fargo to no one in particular.

Fargo's thoughts were suddenly interrupted by Henry Fant, who asked if he wanted another whiskey. Before Fargo could reply, both men were suddenly distracted by a loud angry shout from the table in a dark corner at the opposite end of the saloon.

"Hey, barkeep, drop what you're doin' and bring us another round of beers over here!"

Fargo turned slowly and regarded the shouter. The young man, seated at the table against the wall with three other youths, was no more than seventeen years old. The sparse growth of blond beard on his chin accentuated his boyishness, but the two Colts he wore on his hips suggested he believed he was anything but. Even in the dim light of the room, Fargo could see three notches carved into the wooden handle of one of the revolvers.

Ignoring the youth and turning back to Fant, Fargo said, "Let me have one more whiskey before I go see if I can get into that card game."

As Fant poured from the bottle, the young shouter rose, kicked back his chair and, with an arrogant scowl on his face and arms extended slightly away from his holstered revolvers, stormed up to Fargo.

Though he was at least eight inches shorter than Fargo, the youth glared angrily at the newcomer. "I don't know who you are, mister, but when Amos

Moody calls for a beer, ain't nobody better get in the way. Better men have tried and they're buried out yonder behind this saloon."

As Fant hastily drew four beers, he leaned across the bar toward Moody and said, "Amos, I think there's somethin' you ought to know about this stranger. This here is . . ."

"Shut up, Fant," said Moody. "I'll ask you when I need your advice."

Fant glanced fearfully in the direction of Fargo and then slowly backed away to the far end of the bar.

Fargo sighed deeply and said, "Look, friend, all I want to do here is enjoy a nice, quiet drink. How about if you go sit back down with your pardners and leave me alone?"

"It look's like I'm gonna have to teach you some manners, mister," Moody said, still scowling.

The youth stepped backward two short paces and moved his hands closer to his revolvers.

Fargo, growing aggravated at the empty, tough talk from the youngster, moved one hand closer to a revolver. "I think you need to go sit down before you get hurt, sonny," he said.

When Fargo turned back toward the bar to take a sip of his whiskey, Moody grabbed him by the shirt and yanked him back around. Glaring up into Fargo's face, Moody said, "Look at me when I'm talkin' to you, mister, or I'm liable to put a bullet between your eyes." Moody's right hand rested nervously on the handle of one Colt.

Faster than a lightning strike, Fargo's left arm shot out, his hand seizing Moody's right wrist and holding it immobile on the gun. As he tightened his grip on the wrist bones, Moody grimaced in unexpected pain.

Cocking his right hand far back behind his ear, Fargo shot his huge fist forward, meaty knuckles smacking into Moody's forehead with a sickening thud. The youth dropped like a poleaxed bull.

"Consider yourself lucky, sonny," Fargo said, looking down at the unconscious Moody. "Most men wouldn't let you off so easy."

Seeing their companion fall to the floor, the three toughs jumped from their seats, simultaneously grabbing for their pistols.

In an instant, Fargo flashed iron. He drew both Colts from his belt, and pointed them toward the trio. The quickest of the three managed to squeeze off a single shot that tore through the deerskin of Fargo's shirtsleeve near the right shoulder. Before any of the gunmen could fire again, Fargo placed three slugs into Quick Draw's chest, slamming the stunned shooter back against the adobe wall. Already dead, he slid to the floor, the blood oozing from his exit wounds, streaking the pale mud behind him.

A moment's hesitation would prove costly for the other young gunhawks, frozen in shock over their fallen partner. One slower than the other, they freed their guns and tried to take aim. Their frantic motion was a useless gesture, their fates sealed the moment they decided to try and take a shot at the Trailsman. Before either of them could let loose a single shot, a thin line of flame spat from Fargo's twin barrels as he fired repeatedly. Two crimson holes, spaced only an inch apart, opened up on the face of the one on the right. As he toppled to the floor, two more slugs tore through the stomach of the one on the left, leaving him flopping around in pain on the floor, until a third and final shot put him out of his misery.

The smell of gunsmoke filled the silenced room.

Holstering his revolvers, Fargo drained the remaining whiskey from the glass.

As he set the tumbler back onto the bar, Fargo felt a heavy hand on his shoulder. Turning, he looked directly into the eyes of the gambler in the big hat.

"That's some mighty fancy shooting, stranger. If you'd care to see if you're as lucky at cards as you are with guns, we've got an empty seat at my table you're welcome to occupy."

Returning the gaze, Fargo said, "Luck had nothing to do with it, but I'll accept your invitation anyway."

Without extending a hand, the gambler introduced himself. "My name's Frank Ormsby. I might have some work for a man with your talents with a gun."

"I'm Skye Fargo," he replied, "and I ain't lookin' for a job."

"Skye Fargo," laughed Ormsby, the sound of a deep rumble rolling up from his chest. "Same name as that famous trail guide?"

"Something like that," Fargo replied.

As Ormsby strode back to the table, the bartender called Fargo aside. "Them boys you just killed are the Moody brothers."

Pointing to the prone figure on the floor, Fant continued. "Amos, who's gonna wake up with a mean headache, is the youngest of the lot. The dead ones are Clyde, Barney, and Porter."

Bystanders began carrying the dead bodies out of the saloon as Fant spoke.

One of the cardplayers who quit Ormsby's poker game earlier walked up and spoke to Fant. "Marshal Thompson's due to arrive back from El Paso today. I'll tell him what happened here when he arrives."

The cardplayer then grabbed Amos Moody's heels and dragged the limp form out the front door.

Glancing back over at the poker table where Ormsby was dealing a fresh hand, Fargo said, "Excuse me. I think I'm gonna play cards."

Frank Ormsby won the first two games of five-card draw. During the third game as the gambler was reaching for a card, Fargo's left hand shot forward in a blinding movement and seized the big man by the wrist. Sharply twisting his forearm and giving it two hard and painful shakes, Fargo dislodged an ace of clubs from Ormsby's sleeve.

Glaring into Ormsby's eyes, Fargo said, "You're not only a trail predator, you're a damned card cheat to boot." As Fargo spoke, his right hand slid under the table, his fingers curling around the walnut grip of his Colt. He pulled it from his belt and positioned it out of sight with the barrel pointing toward Ormsby's chest.

The two other gamblers at the table cast nervous glances at Fargo and Ormsby. They both pushed back from the table, then cautiously rose from their chairs and disappeared into the gathering crowd.

Grimacing at the pain of Fargo's grip that was surging through his arm, Ormsby said, "You have me confused with someone else. I ain't never been no trail thief."

"That's a mighty strange coincidence." Fargo smiled as he set the trap. " 'Cause the last time I saw that hat it was attached to a running scared coward, too yellow to check on his own gang. Then again, maybe it's best that it wasn't you, considering how I took them all down after they tried to kill me on the road south of the border."

"You!" Ormsby's startled response convinced the onlookers of his guilt. They had heard about the activities of the horse thieves operating in Mexico for months, but until now they had no idea Ormsby was one of them.

Fargo released his grip on the gambler's wrist, and still holding the Colt under the table, he leaned back in his chair.

"You're a snake, Ormsby," Fargo snarled. "You're worse than a back shooter because you won't give anyone a fightin' chance. You prefer to kill a man while he's sleeping."

The big man jumped up and jabbed a finger in Fargo's direction. "You've gone too far, mister. I aim to kill you for that."

As Ormsby reached for his pistol, Fargo grinned and said, "Before you try, I'm gonna tell you something."

Pausing, Ormsby said, "What's that?"

"I'll kill you before you clear leather."

Ormsby's eyes widened with the realization of what he just heard. Determined to beat the flow of terror creeping through his being, he yanked the revolver from the holster.

Just as Ormsby's barrel cleared leather, Fargo pulled the trigger on the pistol he held out of sight. The middle of the poker table shattered in an explosion of splinters as a single slug tore through the wood and into the center of the gambler's chest.

Ormsby, still clutching the handle of his gun, staggered sideways toward the window, the barrel of Fargo's revolver following his movement.

With great difficulty, Ormsby muttered the words "Skye Fargo" through a froth of blood dribbling out of the corners of his mouth. The dying man made another attempt to draw his revolver. As his hand tightened around the grip, Fargo shot him once more, the impact of the lead ball driving the burly man backward through the window and into the narrow alley beyond.

Rising from the chair, Fargo was holstering his Colt when a deep voice behind him said, "Don't make a move, mister, or there won't be enough of you left to feed the coyotes. Raise those hands high above your head."

The saloon patrons that clustered around the shattered window to look at the sprawled and bloody figure of Frank Ormsby turned to watch this new development.

"Now," said the deep voice, "turn around slowly and keep your hands as close to the ceiling as you can get them."

Turning about, Fargo found himself looking into the craggy face of a man as tall as he with shoulders almost as broad. Spotting a badge pinned to his vest, Fargo wondered if he was about to be arrested. Instead, the lawman lowered the shotgun he was aiming at Fargo and introduced himself as Marshal Emmett Thompson.

Breaking into a smile, Thompson said, "I heard your name is Skye Fargo," and proffered a hand.

Fargo lowered both of his and extended one to Thompson. "How do you know who I am?"

"A man's reputation rides a faster horse than he does," Thompson replied. "I talked to your friends outside, the fur trapper and the priest. They told me who you was."

Pointing toward the broken window, Thompson said, "Somebody ought to pin a medal on you for killing Ormsby. We've tried to catch him and his gang at robbing and killing lone travelers but haven't had much luck. It was just a matter of time before he tangled with someone who could fight back."

"You'll find part of his gang in a cottonwood grove about two weeks' ride south of here," said Fargo. "They're all dead."

Nodding, Thompson said, "We're grateful for that. I was told you were scoutin' in a canoe this time. From the stories I've heard, I thought you and that horse of yours was married to the land."

"This is the easiest way to find what Mr. Brooks is lookin' for . . . a place to run trap lines on the upper Rio Grande."

Thompson nodded as he turned to leave. "Best you be real careful north of here. That's Mimbres Apache country, an' their new chief, Mangas Coloradas, ain't all that friendly toward strangers."

"We'll be on the lookout for 'em, and for that chief," Fargo said. "My friends and I had planned to spend the night here, but in light of what just happened with all this gunplay, I think I'll make arrangements for a horse for the priest and we'll continue on our way."

"Suit yourself, Fargo," Thompson said. "This land still belongs to Mexico. I've got no legal jurisdiction here. You killed men who drew on you first. That's self-defense in my book."

6

Without a trail to follow, Father Olivares could only travel at a snail's pace, picking his way around stands of oak and cottonwood where his cart was too wide to make it through. The bay gelding Fargo bought for Olivares pulled steadily enough, but the going was rough. Keeping the priest in sight required that they paddle slowly, although the potential benefits of having someone who spoke a few words of the Indians' tongue far outweighed the slight delays Olivares might cause them.

"He'll be able to help us make a deal," Fargo said. "At least they'll be able to understand what we want from 'em. And I don't figure he'll be any trouble. Sharin' our food with him won't amount to much. Come sundown we'll see if we can hunt up a wild turkey roost or maybe a deer."

Josh nodded. "He seems likeable enough, but he sure as hell don't have no gift for travelin' through this country. He's near starved down to skin an' bones. That was mighty generous of you to buy him that horse when his donkey pulled up lame. If you ask me, he should'a stayed in Mexico City."

"I'll agree he don't seem to belong here. But if you asked him, I'm sure he'd tell you it was a blessing in disguise," Fargo laughed.

* * *

Father Olivares seemed in high spirits as they prepared their evening meal at dusk. Josh managed to land another big yellow cat with a hook and grubworm, pan-frying slices of fish while a pot of beans bubbled softly over the fire. Evening shadows deepened beneath cottonwood limbs around their camp as the priest shared his thoughts on the Indians. Rummaging through his packs until he found a tattered leather-bound book.

"I do believe Father Augustine mentioned that they ate parts of some animals raw," he said, untying a piece of discolored blue ribbon holding the pages closed, his sunburned face twisted into lines of concentration.

"Just the liver," Fargo told him, shaking his head in a way that clearly conveyed his impatience for ignorance. "Many tribes take the liver right out of the carcass while the buffalo's still kickin'. It's a sign of respect and tradition."

Josh merely listened, watching the river as Olivares spoke again.

"Tradition or not it does seem a rather revolting practice." He began turning pages carefully. "I'm quite sure Father Augustine mentioned that, and several other practices, like the removal of a lock of hair from the heads of their enemies."

"It ain't just hair," Fargo remarked. "They cut off the skin attached to the skull along with it."

The priest's color paled somewhat. "One cannot expect them to understand heathen practices until they have been taught the word of God, Mr. Fargo. This is why we have been sent to them, in order to teach them how to live a God-fearing, civilized way of life.

Franciscans take an oath to devote their lives to spreading the word of God among those who do not know of God's existence. Under the leadership of Father Augustine we shall build a mission among them and show them the pathway to eternal life."

Josh grunted. "You may find out this Father Augustine an' his followers never got the chance to teach 'em nothin'. If it didn't go the way they planned buildin' that church, they could wind up bein' dead."

Olivares looked across the flames at Josh. "We were prepared to give our lives, as did my companion, Father Esteban. If God has chosen us to make this sacrifice, then it is His will and we accept it." He returned to his book, turning pages one at a time. "Before we assume Father Augustine has failed, we must find this river he mentions coming from the northwest."

"First off, we've gotta find the chief of those Apaches, Mangas Coloradas, so we can explain why we're here. While you're talkin' to 'em, you can ask about Father Augustine and if they know where he built his church. If he got it built at all."

The priest was frowning over a particular page. "There are many Mimbres words with several different meanings. Apparently it can be difficult to know how to use them properly. We studied as many as we could, Father Esteban and I, on our way north from San Antonio. Alas, Father Esteban had a gift for mastering language which I do not, it would seem. If I am to teach them Christianity I must broaden my vocabulary considerably. I lost my companion when the soldiers robbed us, and since then I've had little spirit for mastering the Indian tongue alone." He gave both Fargo and Josh a look. "If you kind gentlemen will allow me to travel the rest of the way with you, I'll be most grateful. Traveling alone in this empty wilderness has been disheartening, to say the least, with no one to talk to."

"You're welcome to stay with us," Fargo said. "Somewhere up this river we'll start lookin' for a crossing so you can get the horse an' cart on the other side. We'll float the wagon on a couple of big logs an' hope the bay can swim to the far side on his own. Stayin' clear of quicksand is gonna be the biggest problem. This river's got more quicksand than most."

The priest nodded vigorously. "I was on the verge of losing my donkey and cart to those treacherous sands when you came along to rescue me. I was too weak to give the poor creature any assistance whatsoever. It was surely an act of God when you appeared round that bend in the river . . ."

"Lady Luck," Fargo offered. "We happened to be at the right place at the right time, I 'spose."

Olivares smiled. "Lady Luck, as you call her, has a name. The Holy Virgin watches over us. We offer prayers to her every single day, asking for her blessings in our daily lives. I will gladly teach you those prayers, gentlemen, so that Mary will also watch over you and keep you from harm."

"Didn't appear this Holy Virgin was doin' much to watch over you back yonder in that quicksand," Josh said, by the tone of his voice showing lack of interest in learning any of Olivares's prayers. "I'd just as soon not get preached to, if it's all the same to you. Never was much on churchgoin'."

"But you see," the priest explained quickly, "the Holy Mother was watching over me. She brought you to that bend in the river at just the right time."

"I'd say it was luck," Josh replied, stirring the fish

to keep it from burning. "But if you believe your Holy Mother is gonna keep us safe, maybe you oughta pray real hard that them Apaches don't decide to lift our scalps when we get where we're goin'."

"I will pray for us all," he said, pausing when his gaze came to something on one of the pages. "The Mimbres have names for different seasons, as we do. They call winter *Pai Aganti*, a time of cold weather coming soon, according to Father Augustine. They have several chiefs, or leaders, depending upon what sort of decision must be made. Before important decisions are made they smoke a mixture of leaves and bark which they call *kinnikinnick*, and they have holy men who see visions telling them what to do. These holy men also keep a sacred idol, called the *taime*, which is a vital part of their sun-dance ceremony. Mimbres worship the sun, moon, and the earth as representatives of their gods. In his diary, Father Augustine believes it will be very difficult to explain Christianity to them because of their limited vocabulary and belief in pagan rituals. Their horse herds serve the same purpose as money. Horses are given, it says here, for all things including the most desirable women. Powerful men in the tribe have several wives, a practice they show little inclination to abandon. As you can see, my work promises to be long and most difficult, bringing God's teachings to a race who worship pagan idols and practice butchery upon their enemies. Both the Mimbres and their enemies, the Comanches, are widely feared by other more peaceful tribes due to their hostility. Both tribes lack written language. They keep a record of their history by drawing scenes on pieces of deerskin, thus our only means of communication will be with words they understand when spoken correctly.

Tonight, and in the days to come, I shall do my best to learn as many as I can."

Fargo stood up as dusk became dark across hills surrounding the river valley. "All we're hopin' you can do is help us tell them we aim to trade beads an' knives for the right to trap beaver here this winter. If you can figure out how to get that said, Josh will be obliged and I can get off this damned river, which'll make me especially thankful as well."

"You have my promise I'll do the best I can. And should I fail to explain things properly, I'm sure Father Augustine will be able to speak for you . . . as soon as we can find him."

Down inside, Fargo believed Father Augustine and his mission among the Apaches had failed.

"Fish's ready," Josh announced. "Beans near 'bout tender enough, too." He placed pieces of fish on a tin plate and gave it to Olivares.

"How can I ever repay your kindnesses?" he said, taking a few spoonfuls of beans from the pot before he began eating hungrily, stuffing his cheeks with food.

"If you can figure a way to explain to those Injuns what we want, that'll be payment enough, Father," Josh said, taking his own plate to the trunk of a tree where he rested his back to eat slowly, watching the last rays of light fade in the west. "But if I was you, I wouldn't count on bein' able to find that other priest an' his workers."

Olivares looked down at his plate. "I have been forced to consider the possibility that Father Augustine and the mission are lost . . . that they met with some ill fate. These things are in the hands of God, my friends."

"Maybe," Josh replied, chewing. "I reckon you

could say it's in the hands of God an' a bunch of Injuns who eat raw liver an' take scalps."

Fargo said nothing, although from what he'd seen so far it was unlikely much of anything would persuade these Apaches to let anyone get what they wanted from this territory without offering them something in exchange. He hoped that glass beads and poorly made knives would be enough.

At sunrise the sky was clear. He'd slept soundly during the night without dreams. As they broke camp after coffee and fried bread for breakfast, Fargo inspected the canoe for leaks and tied their gear down while Josh helped Olivares harness his horse. Dry fall leaves rustled in early gusts of wind passing through limbs above them when they were ready to depart. The priest climbed in his cart and waved before he urged the bay northward.

Fargo took his place at the back of the canoe, wishing he'd ridden his Ovaro stud instead of riding in a bullhide boat, even though the difficult terrain would have been hard on his steed.

7

It was the narrowest spot in the river they'd come to since morning, and when Fargo tested its shallows, he found no quicksand beds that would bog the gelding. They went about gathering dead trees with which to buoy the priest's small cart—it weighed very little and within an hour they had logs lashed to the underbelly and rolled it down to the river to float it across. Josh ferried Father Olivares over in the canoe while Fargo readied the cart and horse for the crossing. Fargo's years scouting the plains for westbound travelers had given him plenty of experience floating wagons across water. The small cart would be no problem if quicksand could be avoided.

Upon Josh's return they led the bay out in the river with a rope tied to its neck. Fargo paddled while the gelding reluctantly began to swim with Josh holding onto the rope to keep it from turning back. The rawboned bay animal swam easily once it struck deep water, and with very little trouble, they soon came to shallows on the east side of the river where the horse could stand.

"Blessed is the name of the Lord!" Olivares cried, taking the rope while the horse shook water from its coat.

Josh grinned. "You might oughta bless that bay's nature because it was willin' to swim without no trouble. Ain't many of the horse family takes to water without persuasion."

Fargo backpaddled their canoe away from shore. "We'll tow the cart across," he said, looking up and down the riverbank. "Keep one eye on the trees, just in case we get visitors before we get back across."

They were able to pull the cart to the east bank without a mishap, although the work was tiring under a blistering noonday sun. It required only a few minutes to harness the horse and in slightly less than two hours after beginning the crossing, they were underway again.

The west bank offered fewer obstacles for the cart, fewer thickets to navigate and gentler terrain in most places. They saw no sign of Indians and with the passage of time, Fargo found himself relaxing. Ahead lay more miles of quiet river winding gently through a shallow, forested valley, which was sprinkled here and there with vast, open meadows deep in drying fall grasses. Off in the distance they could see deep canyons. Now and then, they saw small groups of antelope. The serenity of their surroundings lulled Fargo into a sleepy daze as they paddled slowly along sloping banks lined with cattails and bulrushes. As the sun lowered, fall colors again dazzled his eye with their brilliance. Red and yellow leaves seemed ablaze in trees growing close to the river. Occasional willows spread drooping branches over the water. Towering cottonwoods with fans of bright yellow leaves rose above the rest of the forest near the water's edge. Gusts of soft wind took leaves from many of the branches, sending them twirling off in downward spirals to the forest floor. Fargo reveled in the raw beauty of the scenery as they paddled northward through the river's gentle currents. He listened to the quiet gurgle of paddles and a softer sound made by the prow knifing through slow-moving water.

Not far behind, the priest made relatively good progress on the riverbank, occasionally crossing shallow feeder streams that slowed him down where banks were steep. As the afternoon wore on, some of Fargo's apprehensions over making a trading agreement with the Indians lessened. The silence of the empty river valley made him forget everything else for the present.

As it had for days, the sun turned gauzy as it lowered into a thin haze hovering above the earth before sunset, and with it came a subtle change in the colors around them. Again, the river turned bloodred, shimmering in slanted sunlight as though some endless crimson ribbon had been laid across the land. As darkness approached they saw more and more wild animals coming to the river to drink . . . a small herd of doe with a wary buck standing back in the forest, until the sounds of Olivares's cart sent them bounding away into the trees.

Josh pointed to a small clearing at the water's edge. "If we made camp there, we'd have a view on all sides. Looks like there's plenty of grass for the horse, too."

Fargo looked upriver a moment. "Can't see anything looks no better up yonder. Let's head for shore an' wait for the priest to catch up. Everything considered, after the crossin' we made, I figure we made pretty good time today. No sense gettin' a big hurry."

They swung their canoe for shore. Off to the east, Father Olivares's cart rattled over a section of rough ground little more than a quarter mile away. As the canoe edged to a halt in soft mud beside the river-bank, Fargo felt thankful for an uneventful day without encountering any more Indians. He wondered if the priest had anything to do with it, praying to his Holy Mother for their safe journey. It was possible, he supposed, that someone other than Olivares himself had been looking out for them. There was no better explanation for the fact that Olivares was still alive, as ill equipped as he seemed for surviving in this wilderness.

Seated around their campfire, Olivares read from the diary as crickets and bullfrogs sang their songs to the night. "The Apache word for trade is *nodemah*. In order to ask, 'How are you, friend?' it must be pronounced, *hi, hites*. It would appear from Father Augustine's writings that to correctly say you wish to trade with them, you would first say, '*Hi, hites. Coon-ah nodemah.*' "

Fargo said it to himself, thinking how similar it was to the Ute tongue. "How do we tell 'em we want to give beads an' knives for furs?"

"It may be difficult," the priest replied, scowling down a page. "The word for knife is *we-iti*. I am unable to find a word for beads or jewelry. As to explaining that you want beaver fur in exchange for those items, it may best be accomplished showing them what you want. Alas, there is no word listed for beaver or pelts of any kind. There is one notation here . . . a white man is called *Tosi*." He glanced up at Josh. "A black man is called *To-oh Tivo*. Being Spanish and a priest, they will call me *Powva*. I am afraid there isn't much else we can use here to tell them what you want, however when we do find Father Augustine I'm quite sure he'll be able to explain it."

"That's if you find him," Josh said. "If they ain't killed him by now."

Olivares closed the diary and looked down at his worn sandals for a moment. "I believe God has seen to their safety and the building of the mission. Father Augustine lived among the Mimbres Apaches for some time before he wrote this account for the bishop. If they meant to harm him, it would seem they would have done so as soon as he arrived."

Fargo turned his attention to the river. An unknown distance to the west lay beaver country, and judging by the way the Apaches and Comanches watched them enter their territory, a time might come when he and Josh had to choose between running away or fighting to the death. He had his doubts as to whether Josh could accomplish his fur trapping this winter without difficulty, knowing that he would be on his own. As soon as they found beaver territory, Fargo was headed back to El Paso to round up his mustangs and head for Colorado before the snows got too deep. He had told Josh this from the beginning, he just hoped he'd be able to do it when the time came.

They were paddling near the mouth of a creek feeding into the river when Fargo abruptly stopped rowing, looking upstream. Early morning shadows still lay like murky puddles below trees lining the banks of the creek as the sun rose slowly behind them. In the wake of their canoe tiny whirlpools flattened as the current swept them away toward a golden sunrise, reflecting warm yellow light off the river as though it was a piece of glass.

"I heard somethin'," Fargo warned quietly, "like voices. I know I didn't imagine it. Sounded like somebody was laughin'."

Josh craned his neck to see upstream around a bend where the creek narrowed. "I don't hear anything," he said.

Water burbled past the canoe's prow. All was quiet until a blue jay cried and flew from a willow branch near the bank.

"There it is again," Fargo whispered, "comin' from that creek yonder, only it's way off. I just barely heard it that time."

In the distance Josh thought he could hear water splashing, a waterfall's sound. "I can't hear nothin' besides this river an' maybe a waterfall up the creek a ways. I sure never heard nobody laughin'."

They floated closer to the small creek's mouth. The stream was scarcely a dozen yards wide and shallow, looking to be no more than a couple of feet deep in the middle with gently sloped banks lined with slender oak and cottonwood. They could see upstream only a short distance before a bend obscured the creek's course from view. Fargo doubted the priest would have any difficulty crossing it in his cart.

Then he heard it again and this time it was distinct, the sound of laughter, a woman's voice.

"It's a woman," Josh said, cocking an ear, confirming what Fargo thought he heard.

It did sound like a girlish giggle coming from around the bend. "It is a young-soundin' voice, ain't it?" he added. Another burst of laughter came from the bend and the voice was different, slightly higher than the first. "More'n one, too. Figures to be Injun girls. Can't hardly be nobody else."

Josh's curiosity began to get the best of him. "Row over to the bank real quiet. We'll slip through those trees an' have ourselves a look."

"Might not be such a good idea. Where there's Injun women there's liable to be Injun men."

"We'll go careful . . . won't get too close." Josh swung the aft of the canoe around and started paddling into the stream before Fargo could voice any more objections. Girlish laughter continued to echo among trees lining the creek bank.

They paddled slowly toward a stand of cattails, listening to more laughter somewhere to the north. Fargo, accepting their detour and more than curious himself by now, pointed to the cattails and whispered, "We'll hide the canoe in there. Be sure you bring your rifle, just in case we run into more than we bargain for."

The bullhide boat slid quietly among the cattails and came to a halt in mud and sand. Fargo stepped out, feeling his boots fill with water where the lasts had pulled away from stitching.

Cradling their rifles, they beached the canoe among tall reedlike leaves with fuzzy brown flower spikes and waded ashore.

"This way," Josh said quietly, hunkering down to creep among scrub bushes and undergrowth beside the water, carefully placing each foot so it made as little sound as possible.

Fargo fell in behind, listening to the voices ahead. Several girls were laughing, and now he could hear water splashing back and forth as if they were playing while bathing in the stream.

They moved quietly to the spot where the creek made its turn westward. Josh crouched even lower as he shouldered through a tangle of tall grass and branches to the base of a cottonwood on a little knoll above the creek bank.

As Josh was peering around the cottonwood trunk, all noises coming from the stream stopped suddenly . . . there was no more of the splashing sounds and the laughter abruptly ended. Before Fargo could get a look himself, Josh quickly drew back behind the tree and held a finger to his lips.

"They saw me," he whispered, "and they's runnin' into them woods yonder. Be best if we clear out of here before they bring back some of their menfolk."

Fargo started inching backward. "Who were they? Did you get a look at them?"

Josh gave what might pass for a grin. "Injun girls, naked as the day they was borned. Five or six of 'em. Wasn't enough time to get a count." He moved quickly away from the tree as Fargo hurried back toward their canoe in a crouch. "They didn't have a stitch of clothes on, and damned if they wasn't a pretty sight, bathin' in that pool."

Hearing about naked Indian maidens bathing in a pool brought Fargo a rich cloud of memories. He'd been without a woman for many months. For most of his adult life, beginning at age fourteen, he had sought the company of women, wherever he could find them.

Fargo reached the canoe first and pushed it into deeper water before he climbed in, placing his rifle near his feet as he took the paddle. Josh swung easily into the boat while Fargo rowed them backward away from the cattails.

"How'd they look?" he asked, taking deep bites with his oar until they were well away from shore.

"Pretty as angels," Josh replied, swinging the prow with powerful strokes and soon they were gliding into the main course of the river. "One was sittin' on a rock watchin' over the rest of 'em. She saw me, or heard me, an' she clapped her hands just once. They all took off runnin' into them trees like they wasn't ever gonna stop. Before you could blink twice, they was gone out of sight."

Fargo conjured up a vision of naked Indian girls bathing in a stream. "Sure wouldn't have minded a look myself," he said as they turned the canoe sharply to the west.

Josh chuckled softly. "You'd be like me if you'd laid eyes on 'em, willin' to trade every string of beads an' ribbon we got for just one."

Faint stirrings in Fargo's groin made him wonder if Josh was closer to the truth than he knew. It seemed like such a long time ago when he was with a woman . . . when he was happy, content, before this damned river got to him.

8

False dawn brightened the eastern sky. Fargo crept up to the stream without his rifle, carrying nothing but the knife in his belt and the derringer in his boot.

Hiding behind cattails, he crouched down and waited. He'd told Josh that he felt it was necessary to scout around the bank where they had found the Indian women. The men of their tribe might not be far away. Scouting was definitely the best plan, but he certainly wouldn't complain if he caught a glimpse of the bathing beauties.

At first, he thought the bathing spot was empty. He let out the breath he was holding. It would have been a stroke of luck to find the Indian girls back at the same place, but none the less he was hopeful . . . until now.

And then he saw a lone Indian seated on a flat rock beside the creek. She had a bundle of clothing near her feet, all manner of skins decorated with tiny beads and the claws of wild animals.

Fargo watched her from hiding for several minutes, until at last the young woman began putting the clothing items into the water below the rock.

More light came from the east, and now he could see that she was slender, small in stature, with an oval face and long dark hair falling over her shoulders. Very pretty, wearing a simple deerskin dress that was deeply stained.

The girl placed the clothing in the water, then she stood up slowly and pulled her dress upward, over her head. Fargo stared in amazement. The Indian maiden had large, pendulous breasts and a very small waist, with rounded hips ending at the tops of perfectly shaped thighs.

"Damn," he whispered, wondering what to do.

If he made a move toward her, he felt sure she would run away . . . and possibly bring back warriors from her tribe. Fargo knew the customs and ways of many tribes, but this group hidden along the river was clearly foreign to him. Even if they were Apache or Comanche, they were of no sect that he had ever run across. He wondered idly if perhaps he should have ridden on to Colorado Territory with his mustangs. Two hundred dollars was not worth dying for, although he'd faced the fiercest tribes and meanest outlaws in other parts of the West and come out clean.

The girl stepped into the stream. She began to wash the skins and her dress.

Fargo carefully examined the cottonwoods lining the creek to see if more Indians were there. He found nothing but early-morning shadows . . . he heard only the chirping of birds and the splashing sounds the girl was making as she soaked the animal skins and rubbed them together.

Taking a chance, he stood up and began a silent approach to the bank of the creek.

The Indian saw him almost at once and went rigid.

Fargo gave the sign for peace. "I am a friend," he said in English.

The girl's smooth brow knitted. "You . . . be . . . a . . . priest?" she stammered, suddenly showing fear.

Fargo chuckled. "I'm no priest, just a friend. How is it you know my language?"

"I learn . . . from a man like you."

"I won't harm you," he said, halting a few yards away from her, his eyes momentarily drawn to her generous breasts. "I give you my word."

"You go now. Is wrong . . . you see me like . . . this. Is forbidden."

"I couldn't help myself. You're so beautiful."

"Go now. No look at me."

"If that's what you want, but I'd sure like to stay a while if you'll allow it."

"Is wrong."

Fargo started to turn. "I only wanted to take a bath in this creek. I need a bath real bad."

"You are the one who came . . . before," she said, covering her rosy nipples with her hands.

"Yes. My friends and I were going up the river. We didn't mean to disturb you."

"Go away now. If . . . Mangas comes, he kill you for . . . look at me."

"Mangas Coloradas?"

"He . . . chief of our people."

"Then you're a Mimbres, an Apache."

She merely nodded, backing into the stream so that the soft swirl of pubic hair at the tops of her thighs was covered with water.

"My friends and I would like to talk to Chief Mangas, to offer him gifts in exchange for trapping beaver."

"What is beaver?" She had trouble saying the word.

"Animals that chew down trees. My friend wants them for their fur."

"*Okai*," the girl said.

"I don't know what to call them in Apache, but we bring many gifts for Chief Mangas and his people."

"You must . . . make talk with Mangas. I am only a woman. Mangas must decide."

"What is your name?"

"Chokole," she replied softly.

"That's a pretty name. My name's Skye."

"Skye?"

"I know. It's a bit unusual."

"Go." She said it with less resolve this time.

"I'll walk downstream a little way and take my bath, then I'll go away," he said, feeling heat in his abdomen when he saw her silky body in better light, with the sun rising behind them now.

He walked closer to the joining of the Rio Grande and the creek, where he stopped to take off his ammunition belt and knife. Then he slithered out of his deerskin shirt so that his muscles glistened as he bent down to put the garment on a patch of grass.

Lastly, he sat down and pulled off his boots, being careful to leave the toothpick in place before he shucked off his buckskin pants, leaving himself completely naked.

From the corner of his eye, he saw Chokole watching him, and his stiffening member.

"You cover!" Chokole protested.

In an act of feigned modesty Fargo turned his back on her as he wadded into the shallows. He grinned to himself, for he could tell Chokole was interested, or showing at least some interest, in what was hanging between his legs.

"Sorry," he mumbled. "All I want to do is wash some of this dust off me."

"If Mangas comes . . . he will kill you."

"I'm takin' that chance, Chokole. Like I said, all I want is a bath, an' to wash my buckskins."

"You dress like Indian," she said.

He knelt down in the water. "I've been out west most of my life. Ain't too many places where a man can buy denims or sackcloth shirts, not way out here."

"Do you have . . . a woman? I do not know the white man's word."

"You mean wife? Nope. Never found one that suited me all that much."

Chokole looked away and resumed washing her laundry, but now her breasts were exposed.

"You're a downright pretty lady, Chokole," he said, making it sound like an idle remark.

She ignored him.

"Tell me again where you learned English?"

"The old priests. They came up this river. They tried to teach our people about your god."

"What happened to them . . . these priests."

"Our enemies kill them. The white priests bring a sickness with them. Kill many Apaches. Many Comanches."

"How long ago was that?"

"Many *taums*."

"Several years?"

"I do not know word . . . years. Many moons."

Fargo was certain she meant years. "Can your people take us to this place where the priests were killed?"

"Is not for me . . . to say. Chief Mangas must say."

"Can I . . . can we talk to him?"

"He will kill you if he finds you here."

Fargo turned to face her. "Chief Mangas isn't here now, so we can do whatever we want."

Chokole stopped washing her garments. "What is it you want?"

"You," he replied, grinning.

When she smiled, he began walking toward her through the mud and shallow water.

His member pulsed inside her. She dug her fingers into the soft clay below a cottonwood tree.

"It feels . . . good," she breathed, panting.

Her moist mound opened wider for him. He pushed another inch of his shaft into her wetness.

"It is so . . . big," Chokole cried. "Is wrong for me do this," she gasped, hunching against the base of his shaft while she said it.

"It's not wrong when a man and a woman are attracted to each other."

He began driving his pole into her depths, and now Chokole closed her eyes.

"Feels good," she hissed between clenched teeth.

"I told you it was all right," he said, feeling an explosion rise deep within his loins.

She went stiff underneath him while he had one of her nipples in his mouth.

"Good! Good!" she gasped.

Chokole reached her climax only moments before Fargo reached his own. For a time they remained locked in each other's embrace, straining to achieve the full extent of their passion.

Suddenly, Chokole went slack. She was panting for air as fast as she could.

"That felt mighty good to me," he said, resting most of his weight on his elbows.

"I go now," she said, when her eyes opened. "The other women will be coming."

Fargo drew his member out of her, feeling better than he had in weeks. "Whatever you say, pretty lady. Just remember to ask Chief Mangas if we can talk to him. We'll show him the beads, and iron knives, some pretty pieces of cloth."

"I do not understand these words."

"We'll show you. Just talk to Mangas for us. We'll be movin' upriver, but be sure you tell him we come in peace, that all my friend wants is the beaver skins."

Chokole scrambled to her feet. As Fargo was standing up to fetch his clothing, the Apache girl got dressed and grabbed her garments from the edge of the creek. In seconds, she was gone.

9

They'd talked about women most of the morning, a result of sighting the Indian girls bathing. Fargo said nothing about his meeting with Chokole. He meant to save what he'd learned about Mangas Coloradas for later, when the occasion arose.

Josh recalled a Creole girl he knew in New Orleans named Anne, who worked the cribs on backstreets near the wharfs for a modest living. He'd become a regular caller of Anne's, and as time passed they became better acquainted, then friends. Anne became his lover and they even spoke of marriage, until a trip up the Mississippi took Josh away for nine weeks. When he returned there was neither sign, nor word of where she might have gone.

"She couldn't leave me a note because she never learned how to write," Josh remembered, finishing his story with a touch of sadness in his mellow voice. "I truly had a fondness for that gal. She had the most beautiful body you ever saw, and her cookin' was near 'bout the best I ever tasted. I reckon I'll always wonder what come of her. Her dresses an' such was gone from the wardrobe. Maybe it was only that I was away too long. That bitch of a river takes a while to pole. I've told myself a thousand times it was the Mississip' that took Anne from me. I blamed the river, only it was me that was gone for so long."

Josh saw an eagle land in the highest branches of an elm overlooking the water. It folded its wings to watch the canoe pass. "There's things about a man's mind most women won't ever understand. I never did understand Anne's way of thinkin' at all. She talked crazy, sometimes, 'bout havin' land of her own an' fields full of cotton. A big house with servants. She never did understand how those things cost a pile of money, more money than she'd make in a lifetime, workin' the cribs."

Suddenly, the eagle shrieked and took off, flying low over the river as though something frightened it, beating its powerful wings until it flew out of sight above the treetops.

"Wonder what spooked that bird?" Josh asked, searching the forest near the tree where the eagle had perched.

For a few moments there was silence, until a distant scream came from the west, a human voice. Fargo froze. It was a woman's scream, and immediately thereafter a chorus of screams arose from the same direction. The cries were clearly those of fear, and now there were so many screams they became like a single noise.

"What the hell . . . ?" Josh scanned the forest ahead and saw nothing moving.

Fargo couldn't guess. "Let's see what it is. Head for shore an' we'll take a look."

"Maybe it's not such a good idea to stick our noses in where they don't belong."

"Maybe somebody's after those girls we saw at the creek. Whatever it is, somethin's damn sure happening or they wouldn't be yelling like that." Fargo swung the canoe for shore and paddled as hard as he could, thinking of Chokole the entire time.

They reached the riverbank and jumped out with their rifles and pistols in hand. Fargo took off in a run through a canebrake and then a thicket of oak while Josh was securing the canoe to a limb. Dodging back and forth in the forest, he heard one of the women yelling words he couldn't understand and then she screamed, her voice trailing off into a series of gasping moans.

He reached an opening a quarter mile in and stumbled to a halt when he saw a sight that brought him up short. In a clearing just beyond the trees, dozens of strange, dome-shaped dwellings sat in the sunlight. Several mounted Indians galloped among the lodges on spotted ponies, while Indian women and children ran in every direction, screaming as the horseback men chased them into the woods or in circles around the tents. Smoldering campfires burned across the Indian camp, making it harder to see what the mounted Indians were doing to the women and children fleeing on foot. For a few seconds Fargo simply stood beside a tree trunk and watched, until an Indian on a black-and-white pony galloped up behind a running girl wearing a deerskin dress. A club in the Indian's right hand swung downward, striking the girl on her head. She groaned and collapsed on her stomach as the mounted Indian galloped his pony past her. More screams came from all across the camp as women and children raced back and forth to escape swinging clubs. Fargo was horrified. Why were these men attacking defenseless women and children?

As one Indian rode his pony around a tent, Fargo

noticed something peculiar about his hair. The warrior wore a pair of braids with an eagle feather tied to it.

"Comanches," he said aloud, remembering violent details attributed to the tribes who meticulously braided their hair into twin braids.

He heard Josh running up behind him as he tucked the Colt into his belt to shoulder his rifle. "Comanches all over the place usin' clubs on women!" he cried, swinging his sights to a mounted Indian. "We got no choice but to take a side with those women an' kids! Shoot the sons of bitches!" As he spoke he thumbed back the hammer. Peering through the V-notch rear sight, he gripped the black walnut stock and gently squeezed the trigger.

His Henry belched flame, slamming into his shoulder with a mighty roar. The Comanche jerked when a ball of lead passed through his side and in the same instant, all the shouting and screaming stopped.

The Indian flew from his pony's withers, driven sideways by the ball's impact. His pony lunged and bounded away, snorting, turning its head toward the unfamiliar sound of gunfire. The Indian tumbled to the ground with a fountain of blood squirting from a hole in his back. And now every eye in the camp was on Fargo and Josh—the Comanches halted their ponies and the women stopped running away from them.

Josh drew a bead on a warrior aboard a prancing white pony and fired. The explosion seemed to rock the trees around them as smoke and fire erupted from the muzzle of Josh's Whitney. The Indian was torn from the back of his horse as though he'd met a mighty gust of wind, spinning him off the pony's rump with his arms and legs flailing, until he landed on his back beside one of the dome-shaped tents and lay still.

As Josh fired, Fargo hurried to reload, forcing a ball and wadding down the muzzle of his rifle with the ramrod's brass tip.

The echo of a second gunshot faded. Every Indian in the clearing was staring at the trees where Fargo and Josh stood. An eerie silence spread over the camp and for a few moments, as Fargo fitted a percussion cap on the nipple, not one Indian moved or made a sound. Two loose ponies trotted off into the woods, one with blood covering its rump and flanks.

"Don't shoot no more, Skye," Josh whispered. "Look what's happenin' . . ."

Mounted Comanches turned their ponies, pointing at the trees as they began shouting unrecognizable words to each other. Three of them took off in a gallop, riding as hard as they could away from the tents and heading north. They disappeared into a cluster of thick oak and elm at the edge of the clearing. The others followed, drumming heels into their ponies' ribs, and in less than half a minute every one of the Comanches had ridden away, leaving their dead behind.

Fargo took a deep breath. "Whatever was goin' on, I couldn't just let 'em club those women an' children. These women are most likely Mimbres, an' it appeared they was bein' raided by Comanches, maybe while their menfolk were off huntin'. I couldn't just sit an' watch it. I had to take a side with these women."

Josh was looking at the women. The ones who hadn't hidden in the forest merely stood in plain sight, watching Josh and Fargo in silence.

"Maybe you got it figured right, only it seems like they's afraid of us. No way to make 'em understand why we came to help. They don't understand us an' we sure as hell don't know how to understand what they're sayin'."

"I figure none of 'em ever heard a gun go off before. It's the noise that's got 'em scared."

Josh relaxed his grip on his rifle. "It didn't hurt none that we shot two of the bastards who was botherin' 'em. Maybe that'll count for somethin'."

"I've got an idea," Fargo said, resting his rifle against his leg. "If we put some beads an' ribbon out in plain sight an' then get back on the river like we aimed to mind our own business, that oughta show 'em we don't mean no harm."

One of the women, wearing a badly stained deerskin dress, crept cautiously over to the woman who had fallen from a blow to the head by a Comanche. She knelt, still keeping a wary eye on the two strangers, to touch the downed woman's shoulder. Slowly, a few at a time, more women came from the trees and tents to stare at Fargo and Josh. Somewhere behind one of the tents, a child began to cry. Smoke from the fires drifted across the clearing, making it harder to see any of the Indian women on the far side who were still close to the woods.

"No reason for us to stay any longer," Josh said. "Let's clear out of here before the Apache menfolk show up. It don't appear none of them Comanches want any more of our guns."

"I'll keep an eye on things here while you head back to the canoe and bring back what we need," Fargo offered, "just in case." He looked for Chokole among the women but couldn't find her.

Josh nodded and turned for the river. Fargo watched the women stare at him, wishing there was something he could say to them to let them know they wouldn't be harmed. Almost as an afterthought he took a few short steps out into the sunlight and held up the sign for peace, keeping his rifle beside his leg.

His movements caused some alarm among some of the women, who backed away when he stepped from the trees. But when he stopped and gave the sign, one young woman standing near a tent said a few words to another girl beside her. The girl looked at Fargo and gave him a slow smile, then she held up her own hand, returning the sign for peace.

"Chokole," he whispered to himself, taking note of how pretty she was. Long black hair fell below her shoulders. Her eyes were a dark chocolate color, and her high cheekbones were covered by pale bronze skin so smooth it appeared flawless. Her short hide dress had designs painted all over it, a running horse, a drawing of the sun, and other symbols he couldn't identify from this distance. He returned her smile, still holding his palm open, and for a few moments they simply stared at each other.

One older woman walked cautiously to the Comanche Josh had shot, peering down at the body. Then she did a strange thing for which Fargo was totally unprepared—she spat upon the corpse and kicked it savagely, saying something under her breath.

Fargo stood rock-still, not wanting to cause fear among the women. He gazed around the camp, taking note of the scattered pieces of clay pottery, and the curious bowl-like shape of the dwellings, but several times his eyes returned to Chokole and his thoughts flashed back to their shared secret. He smiled. She watched him, but now she no longer held up the peace sign, merely standing where she was without taking a step in any direction. Several silent minutes passed and the silence grew uncomfortable.

Josh came up behind him. "Here's two strings of beads an' a length of red ribbon," he said quietly. "Maybe if I hang 'em on a limb of this tree, they'll see we aim to leave presents if we walk away an' get back on the river."

Fargo agreed, nodding. He did not want to clue Josh in on what had happened between himself and the native beauty. For her people such actions, as pleasurable as they were, might bring dishonor or worse. Fargo was familiar with tribes of similar beliefs, and intended to respect them.

Josh placed the beads and ribbon on the end of a low branch where sunlight made the glass beads sparkle. "Let's pull out before anythin' can go wrong. We did what we came here to do. Maybe they'll tell their menfolk what we did an' show 'em our presents. That'll help us make a friendly start with this particular bunch, anyways."

Fargo backed toward the trees, smiling at the pretty young girl one final time, before he lowered his hand and followed Josh back through the forest.

"One of 'em was damn sure a pretty girl," he said quietly, holding back a smile as they walked through the forest and then down to the edge of the river where the canoe was tied.

Josh chuckled, although he continued to glance over his shoulder until they pushed the canoe away from shore. "You got an eye for a pretty gal, Skye, only I wouldn't count none too strong on gettin' a chance to know her."

They climbed in and paddled away from the bank,

moving due west toward a thickly forested section of river valley where the river broadened in the distance.

"All the same," Fargo said, "she sure as hell was a beauty, an' she understood me when I gave her the peace sign." He looked back when he remembered the priest. "I hope Father Olivares stays clear of their camp when he smells smoke. Maybe we oughta double back an' warn him about what's ahead so he'll stay wide of that Indian village."

Josh turned the prow in a slow circle to the east. "Likely he heard the gunshots, anyway. We'd better tell him to stay close so he don't have a run-in with them Comanches himself."

They paddled back downstream looking for Father Olivares, riding easily with the flow of the current.

10

Josh was preparing a feast over their supper fire, roasting a young turkey hen he shot while hunting along the river as the sun went down. Fargo and Father Olivares sat around the flames at dusk while Josh attended to the meal, turning it on a roasting stick above the fire. Fargo was telling the priest what happened at the Indian village, filling in details they hadn't given him when they found him beside the river earlier in the day.

Olivares watched the hen's juices drip into the flames, giving off a wonderful aroma. "It was indeed a wise move to leave them gifts as you departed. They can have no doubts as to your good intentions." He frowned a little. "How odd it is that Comanche men would attack women and children. Father Augustine spoke of all Indian men as warriors, yet it hardly seems fitting for a man who sees himself as a warrior to make war on women. The Apache word for warrior is *vi-ses*, and they apparently take great pride in their fighting skill and bravery. It would seem that Comanche men are not as concerned about showing bravery, using clubs on female Apaches the way you described."

"It goes against my grain when a man beats a woman, don't matter what the reason," Fargo added.

Olivares looked off at darkening hills to the north. "It may have serious consequences, my friends, although I understand why you took action. The Comanche warriors may return to seek revenge for their brethren you killed."

"Let 'em come," Josh said evenly, looking across the flames from hooded eyelids, his deeply lined face taking a savage countenance as he tested the turkey with the tip of his foot-long skinning knife. "If they's lookin' for another fight I've got just the remedy for it. The ones we don't shoot I'll split open like ripe melons." His expression relaxed some. "I don't figure they'll come after us, not after they seen what a Whitney rifle did to their friends. The others ran like scared rabbits when they saw what happened. If they'd wanted a fight, we was right there to oblige 'em. But if they do come back I'll spill their guts all over this ground, so's the dirt's got an excuse for bein' red."

Olivares's face mirrored surprise, even a trace of fear as he listened to Josh. "At first meeting, you seem like such a gentle fellow in spite of your tremendous size, Mr. Brooks. Hearing you now, I see you have another side, a violent side, yet you are so gentle with my donkey and you've shown me nothing but kindness."

Fargo grinned when Josh said nothing. "He's gentle, unless he gets riled. If I were you I wouldn't get in his way when he gets on a mad, 'cause he don't know his own strength an' he sure don't take well to somebody pushin' him. There's a few river pirates down at the bottom of the Mississippi feedin' turtles who wished they'd never tangled with ol' Josh Brooks, according to what I was told."

Olivares swallowed, glancing from Fargo to Josh. "Then you've killed men before?" he asked softly.

Josh gave the priest a chilly stare. "Some, them that had it comin'. Can't recall ever killin' nobody who didn't need a killin'."

Olivares seemed reluctant to pursue the subject further, but he added one more quiet observation. "You should ask God for His forgiveness, Mr. Brooks. If you wish, I'll hear your confession and offer prayers for your eternal salvation. I feel sure you believe there were circumstances requiring you to take the lives of other men."

Josh's irritation was beginning to show. "There damn sure was circumstances, Father, like when some son of a bitch comes at me with a knife or a gun. I don't reckon I need none of your prayers. If the Almighty asks me why I done it, I'll remind Him of those . . . circumstances you was talkin' about. But until there comes a Judgment Day, if there is such a thing, I'm gonna keep on killin' the rotten bastards who need it. Like them Comanche cowards who beat up on those women today. I figure the Almighty was real glad to see us come along when we did."

A bullfrog began its croaking somewhere downriver. Olivares turned his attention to Fargo. "In Father Augustine's diary he warns of a Comanche's hostile nature. Perhaps an Indian war between the Apaches and Comanches will begin over today's encounter. Our lives could be in danger if we are caught between warring Indian tribes."

Fargo listened to the frog a moment. "Not much we can do if that happens, besides stay out of the way. It's been my experience that it's mighty hard to find a place on earth where men ain't tryin' to kill each other. I reckon it don't matter where a man looks for peace, there's always somebody else lookin' for trouble. If they'll allow it, Josh aims to trap beaver in this neck of the woods without givin' those Apaches or Comanches no reason to start a fight. He's offerin' an honest trade with 'em, if somebody can make 'em understand."

"Father Augustine will know how," Olivares assured him, as he edged closer to the fire.

Fargo left it unsaid that he had his doubts they would find a mission or a priest up the river. For now his worries centered around the return of a Comanche raiding party looking for vengeance against the men who interfered with their raid on the Apache camp. He looked across the flames and spoke to Josh. "We shouldn't be too far from the beaver creek by now. I'll take a look at that map later on. There's hardly any landmarks to speak of."

Josh shrugged. "I don't figure the map's done us a bit of good. Damn near every mile of this river looks the same. Back yonder a ways I did see what looked like a low mountain way off to the northwest. Maybe we ain't far from the Guadalupe Mountains. If we don't run into no more trouble with Injuns, maybe we'll see that river's mouth in a few days."

"I'll take the first watch tonight, just to be on the safe side. Let me know soon as that turkey's done. I'm hungry enough to eat the stick runnin' through it." He got up and gathered his ammunition pouch and rifle, looking both ways along the river for a piece of high ground.

"You are expecting trouble from the Comanches, aren't you?" Olivares asked in a tight voice.

"Just bein' careful, Father. A man learns to stay

alive by seein' trouble before it comes." He walked softly into the dark toward a line of trees running east and west on a rise above the river, cradling the Henry in the crook of his arm.

He treaded lightly across fallen leaves and twigs until he found the spot he wanted with a view of the river and hilly land along the north bank. Settling down with his back to a tree, he let his eyes grow accustomed to the darkness. Down below, their fire twinkled in the night, flickering when slow night breezes swept gently across the river. He listened to crickets chirp and an owl's haunting call for several minutes. More bullfrogs up and down the bank croaked endlessly.

He rested his head against the tree trunk, remembering the pretty Apache girl, Chokole. "Maybe things'll work out after all," he muttered softly. Gazing across the river now, he found he was enjoying the night's tranquility, its peace.

Off in the night a coyote barked, then it howled, and the sound was so mournful and lonely it made him feel a touch of sadness. He decided, after a bit, that this land was a place created for solitary men like him, those who sought empty spaces unspoiled by civilization. Parts of the Mississippi had been like that in the beginning, until westward expansion brought towns and farms to more and more miles of its shores. He recalled feeling a trace of sadness then, when there were fewer empty regions to travel. He understood even then he was built differently, seeking solitude rather than the company of others.

"Just a few more days," he whispered, briefly closing his eyes to think about what might lie in store.

11

The land changed slowly as they paddled north, broken by deep gullies twisting through thickly forested hills. More creeks fed into the river now, and along some of the streams they saw beaver sign, gnawed stumps where the animals felled trees to make their dams.

"We're close," Josh said from his vantage point in the prow as they paddled steadily into strengthening currents where creeks added flow to the river. "I can feel it in my bones. We're in beaver country now."

"This is damn sure beaver country. If we wanted, you could set trap lines right here this winter. No tellin' how many damns are up those feeder creeks."

"The best trappin' should be off that big creek," Josh proclaimed. "I've got a feelin' it ain't far to the mouth of it."

Fargo had been examining the surrounding hills for signs they were being watched by Indians. "If you're right, this figures to be the heart of Apache range." He let his gaze wander from one hilltop to the next, pausing where a shadow didn't seem natural. "Sure hadn't seen no trace of an Indian since we left that Apache village. Let's hope those Comanches headed back to their home range. Kinda strange though, they don't seem to be watchin' us like they did."

"They probably hunt buffalo real hard in the fall so's they have meat for the winter. Maybe that explains why none of 'em are around just now . . . both tribes are liable to be off followin' buffalo herds like the one we saw that day."

"Makes sense, I reckon." Fargo glanced back to see how far the priest had fallen behind. "Father Olivares ain't makin' very good time through all these trees." He noted the angle of the sun. "It's nearly noon an' we've already lost sight of him back yonder. Let's find a place to pull out of the water where we can wait for him . . . maybe up the next creek we find with beaver sign. We can walk upstream an' see how big their dams are, maybe get a guess as to how many make up a colony in these parts."

Josh's expression said he wasn't too happy over the delay. "We'd have been there by now if it wasn't for him, only I don't s'pose we coulda just left him where we found him." Squinting in the glare off the river, he pointed west. "Yonder's a creek feedin' the channel. We can tie off an' walk it out . . . see if there's a dam somewheres."

They rowed steadily into the current for half a mile before they came to the stream. Farther up the creek's banks they saw a number of gnawed stumps. Josh aimed the prow for a low spot where marsh grasses grew among scattered cattails and reeds.

The canoe edged into still waters. A fish darted away from the sound of paddles, leaving a telltale swirl near a clump of marsh grass. Josh stepped out and towed the boat ashore before Fargo left his seat carrying his rifle.

"Bring your guns just in case," Fargo said, casting a look up and down the riverbank. "Just because we ain't seen any Indians don't mean they aren't close by."

The walked along the stream, pausing where beavers had chewed down smaller oak and cottonwoods. Narrow beaver trails ran back and forth through thickets on either side of the creek. Moving slow and cautious, they went several hundred yards beside a shallow ribbon of water glistening over rocks where sunlight beamed down through thick branches.

"This creek's mighty small," Josh observed. "Damn near down to a trickle. Those beaver must have built one hell of a dam up yonder some place."

Fargo was paying more attention to the forest. A feeling down the back of his neck had begun to worry him. "Maybe we hadn't oughta go any farther, Josh. Somethin' don't feel quite right around here."

Josh scanned the wooded slopes carefully. "Don't see no reason to worry," he said quietly, balancing the Whitney in his palm, "but if you've taken a notion to go back, it suits me." He took a few more steps toward a bend in the stream. "Look at that big dam, Skye! It's just around the bend. Big, an' as wide as a paddlewheeler. We come this far. Let's have a look."

Still feeling uneasy, he nodded agreement and trudged along behind Josh, keeping an eye on the forest. But when they rounded the bend and saw a massive logjam damming the creek, he forgot all his concerns and grinned. "Let's see how many beaver domes we can count. I see half a dozen from here . . ." He started off in a hurried walk toward the dam, when suddenly, slapping noises came from all sides of a pond created by the logjam. Several beaver had begun to slap their broad, flat tails on the surface of the pool as a warning to the others that danger was near.

"Look at 'em run!" Josh exclaimed, pointing to furry brown animals racing out of thickets near the water, scurrying low to the ground until they splashed into the pool. "Damn! Ain't that a pretty sight?"

Fargo counted eight or nine beaver swimming across the pond toward domes made of mud and sticks floating on the surface. "It is a mighty pretty sight," he agreed, stopping beside an oak tree to continue making his count. "There's better'n two dozen we can see, an' no tellin' how many we missed. You'll be rich as a king, come springtime."

Josh was grinning. "It's like countin' money. Hardly no need to cure coon pelts at two bits apiece when there's so many beaver. Coon's only gonna get in the way, bein' as they's half the price. I'll have to build a log raft big as a house to get all them furs back to New Orleans. It'll be so heavy my biggest worry's gonna be sinkin', furs an' all. This is without a doubt the best beaver country in the world."

Fargo examined a wide clearing around the pool where beaver had taken down virtually every tree. "This dam's been here for a long time," he said. "Nobody came along to disturb 'em while they built it. Trappin' here is gonna be easy, like pickin' corn at harvest time."

Beavers swam toward their domes, cutting tiny wakes across the smooth surface of the pond until they disappeared underwater to hide in their floating nests. Fargo was satisfied. "Let's head back to the canoe. I'll grind up an' boil some of those coffee beans you fried this mornin' until the priest catches up. We're in beaver country, so there ain't no reason to hurry." He gave the pond a final look and sauntered away from the beaver dam with high expectations. He'd done what Josh had hired him to do, taking him to uncharted beaver country. With pelts bringing half a dollar next spring, Josh would amass a small fortune by the time the ice melted.

12

"*We-iti.*" Olivares said the word over and over again as they sat by the fire. It had taken him almost three hours to catch up with Fargo and Josh. "*We-iti,*" he repeated. "I must remember their word for knife. I was never good with languages . . ." He frowned at the pages of the diary.

"You speak right good English for a Spaniard, Father," Josh observed.

"I was educated in English and Spanish. It was the bishop's order that we become fluent in both languages when we were small boys, to prepare us for work in the New World. I was young then, and learning came naturally. As you can see, I have no facility for learning languages now. I have difficulty with my memory."

"How old are you, Father?" Fargo asked, stirring soup made from the last of their turkey meat.

"I am thirty-one this year. I grew up in a monastery in a Mexican village named Saltillo, where young Franciscans prepare for missionary work. Father Esteban and I were schooled together there, which has only worsened my sorrow, having known him most of my life. The Franciscan Order is a way of life for those who take the vows. We were very much brothers to each other . . . the order teaches that we are all like brothers, committed to God's work. Losing my brother and dear friend has been most difficult, but I shall continue our work as though he were at my side."

Olivares turned a page in his book. "Father Augustine writes that Mission Santa Fe is being built up a river coming from the mountains. Twenty leagues from where this river joins the Rio Grande there is a small mountain overlooking the river valley and it is there where I will find them."

"That could be a considerable distance, Father," Josh said. "I 'spect you go most of that distance alone. Me an' Skye are gonna start lookin' for beaver streams off this river, ain't we, Skye?"

Fargo thought about it. "We hadn't planned on goin' twenty leagues upriver, only maybe if we do find this Father Augustine, he'll know more about the country . . . the lay of things where you'd find the best trappin'. Maybe we could go that far up, seein' as it's so early in the fall. Beaver won't start puttin' on thick hair for a month or two, most likely."

"I'd be very grateful if you accompanied me," Olivares said, "and I'm certain Father Augustine will know where the beaver are the most plentiful."

Josh aimed a thumb over his shoulder, in the direction from which they had come. "Can't hardly be no better'n what we saw up that creek today. Beaver was all over the place, an' that creek was hardly more'n a wet spot."

"I'd be willing to bet it gets even better after we find the big creek," Fargo said, relying upon his own memory, as a scout who could read territory like written verse. "Maybe we'll go up a ways, just to see what the river's like. Let's wait an' see how deep it runs."

"I got the feelin' it ain't far," Josh offered, watching his fishing line as the last rays of sunshine beamed into a rose-colored sky. "We saw a few beaver before, but never so many as today. This is beaver country."

The mouth of the river was wide, running deep as though rain had fallen upstream recently, increasing the Rio Grande's flow, which they felt rushing against the canoe for almost an hour before rounding a turn where they found what Fargo believed was the stream they'd been looking for.

"Yonder she is," Josh announced. Far off to the west and north a range of low mountains purpled with haze.

"They shoulda named it the Beaver River," Fargo said, paddling harder to make a swing into the river's mouth against an onrush of muddy water where the rivers joined. Eddies formed in slower backwaters, making for easier rowing when they finally got the canoe turned. "Never saw so much beaver sign in all my days. I gave up countin' stumps a long time ago. There could be more'n a million of 'em here."

Josh's muscular arms glistened with sweat from faster rowing and his sleeveless shirt clung to his back like a second skin in the midday heat. "This river's plenty wide enough for a log raft to haul down our pelts. Plenty of tall trees to make one, too. All we gotta do is make them Injuns understand what we want so's they don't give me no trouble this winter . . ."

Fargo had been watching the riverbank for Indians. "No sign of 'em now. Maybe they understood what

Father Olivares was tryin' to say." He scanned the trees again carefully, making sure. "Hopefully givin' the old man that knife an' those beads did the trick."

Paddling steadily for another quarter hour, they rounded a sharp bend and stopped rowing in unison, when, above treetops in the distance, they saw smoke billowing into a clear sky.

"Sweet Jesus," Fargo muttered. "There must be a hundred fires up yonder." Smoke rose in dozens of swirling columns from a wide area beyond the forest. "We couldn't see 'em before because the trees along this river are so tall an' wind's carryin' the smoke smell away from us."

"It has to be an Injun village, Skye," Josh said, resting his paddle across his lap. "A big one. Sure as hell hope they ain't Comanches."

"Me, too," Fargo added quietly, feeling an unsettling knot form in his gut. "Whoever they are, there's a bunch of 'em. Fires all over the place. When we paddle 'round that next bend, they'll see us for sure. An' this river ain't hardly wide enough for us to stay out of arrow's range." He studied the forest carefully for a moment. Once, he thought he saw a shadow move from one tree trunk to the next. "I think they already know we're here. Somethin' moved over yonder near that big red oak tree just now."

"It'd be natural for 'em to post lookouts close to their village so nobody'd slip up on 'em unannounced. If they's Comanches we could be in for one hell of a fight. The ones we didn't shoot will remember us . . ."

The current began carrying the canoe backward when its slow drift upriver ended. Fargo watched the woods, the glare of sun off water almost blinding him, paying particular attention to the oak tree where he felt sure he saw movement before. The quiet hiss of water against the canoe was the only sound he heard for several minutes. Smoke rose above treetops in thickening spirals beyond the next turn. He felt his heartbeat quickening.

"We can't hardly stop now. This here's the spot we've been headed for ever since we left New Orleans," Josh said. "Only way we're gonna find out what's up yonder is to paddle that direction till we come to it. I say we keep our rifles handy."

When nothing stirred in the forest, Fargo said, "I've got this feelin' we could be makin' a big mistake, but if they've already seen us we've got no choice. Let's keep movin' forward, only paddle real slow and be ready for anything." He picked up his rifle and laid it over his knees to emphasize his point, before he put the paddle back in the water.

Josh resumed paddling. They could see the river narrowing as it made its swing eastward.

Josh dipped his paddle deeper with each stroke. "If any trouble starts, turn this boat around an' paddle hard as you can, Skye. I ain't lookin' for a way to get any more holes in this ol' body than I already got."

Keeping to the far side of the river, they paddled slowly in steady currents past thick brush growing along both banks, places where Indians could hide. Nearing the bend, Fargo was sure he saw shadows moving in the forest now, more than one or two, following their progress upriver.

Long before they began the river's turn, he caught glimpses of fires burning beyond trees lining the bank. And they got a first look at the village moments later, rounding a sandy shoal.

Across a broad, flat meadow, dozens of animalskin

lodges sat in the sunlight. Fargo guessed there could be fifty or more. All across the meadow hundreds of Indians, both men and women, tended to fires below curious wooden racks. Smoldering green wood gave off so much smoke it was hard to see the entire village. But it was easy to see the Indian men waiting for the canoe along the eastern shore of the river. Several dozen men, Apaches by the way they wore their hair unbraided, stood by the edge of the river with bows and arrows and spears, watching Josh and Fargo paddle into view.

Josh stopped rowing. "They don't look friendly, Skye. All of 'em has got weapons, an' they's lookin' at us like they just seen a couple of polecats. We'd best not go no closer."

Fargo's heart was racing and his breathing was shallow. This was a moment he'd been dreading, finding a huge Apache village at the spot where Josh hoped to run trap lines. "These are the ones we have to convince," he said quietly, paddle frozen in his hands as the canoe slowed to a crawl.

Now the canoe began to drift backward with the current. Fargo locked his attention on the men lining the riverbank and he hardly noticed their slow change in direction. None of the Apaches were fitting arrows to bowstrings for the present, although he knew things could change suddenly, without warning.

"I wish that priest was here so he could talk for us," Josh muttered.

"It'll be hours before he catches up," Fargo said, keeping his voice down. "I remember a couple of words. He said *hi, hites* meant, 'hello, my friends,' an' that *nodemah* was their word for makin' a trade. It'll be risky as hell, gettin' close enough so we can talk to 'em. That close, they could fill us full of arrows before we can sneeze, there's so many of 'em."

Josh was thinking out loud. "We can hold up a couple of our knives an' some beads while we paddle to shore. If we gave 'em the peace sign an' you said those words, maybe they wouldn't be so quick to shoot."

"If we're wrong, we're dead men," Fargo warned. "It's takin' one hell of a big chance, but it's your fortune."

Josh turned back to look at Fargo. His oversized, hairless skull glistened with sweat and his face was a mask, without a trace of expression most men could read. His countenance only changed when he was angry. "Take out some of them beads an' a knife or two while I row us toward shore. Hold 'em up so's they can see what we got."

Fargo opened a drawstring pack and took out strings of red and yellow beads and a knife. "Start paddlin'," he said, wondering if he'd just given Josh an order that was about to get them both killed.

13

Seventy-five yards from the riverbank, Fargo and Josh rowed toward a group of thirty or forty Apache men gathering to watch the canoe approach. Fargo could hear a few guttural words being spoken among them. The men wore a strip of animal skin covering their genitals, or leather leggings. Most were bare-chested, but some wore a type of deerskin vest. He searched the faces of the women working near the odd-shaped wood racks, and although he failed to find the girl Chokole, he discovered what the racks were used for. Strips of raw meat lay over a contraption made of small limbs above the flames. Smoke from green firewood surrounded the racks and meat, preserving it, he supposed, for use this winter. But no matter where he looked he found no trace of the Apache girl, the one who had shared her charms with him at the creek, and he concluded that this group was definitely another tribe.

The conical tents across the village bore crudely painted designs and symbols similar to the artwork he'd seen on the girl's dress, drawings of running horses and deer, buffalo, a sunrise. There was no obvious arrangement to the tents, scattered here and there over the clearing as if by happenstance.

Fargo held up the beads and knife to allow as much sunlight as possible to strike them. With the other hand he gave the peace sign, when the distance closed to less than fifty yards. The Apache men showed no recognition and appeared to be paying little attention to the trade items. Josh paddled a few more strokes before crying out, "*Hi, hites. Hi, hites. Nodemah!*"

A stirring occurred among the closest Apaches. They spoke to each other, gesturing toward the canoe. They seemed confused, hearing a man of another race speak their language. Or was it that they didn't understand him at all?

Twenty-five yards from shore some of the men stepped back, while others simply stood there, holding bows without fitting an arrow to the bowstring, showing no signs of aggression.

"*Hi, hites! Nodemah!*" Fargo cried.

Fargo turned the knife and beads to show them clearly what he was carrying, still holding his palm open. They were completely vulnerable to deadly arrows now . . . at the very least, their bullhide canoe would sink quickly from arrow holes near the waterline.

Some Apaches turned when a man emerged from one of the tents. He was slightly taller than the others, more muscular, and his face appeared flatter, more menacing, if Fargo could judge by his expression. He strode toward the water, saying something to one or two of the other men before he reached the riverbank.

Josh shouted, "*Hi, hites! Nodemah!*"

To emphasize what they wanted to trade, Fargo held the items higher. "The big one's some sort of chief," he told Josh, never taking his eyes from the men with bows and spears. "If he gives the order to kill us, it's over."

The smell of smoke drifted across the water when winds made a slight change in direction. The canoe came closer, and now Fargo could see the Indians' faces clearly. They had steeply angled noses, bent down as though they'd been broken, with hard black eyes that never seemed to blink or waver. They watched the men in the canoe warily, but made no show of hostility.

Josh braked the canoe to a halt with his paddle, letting it sit still for a moment. "*Hi, hites. Nodemah.*"

The tall Apache came to the edge of the river, staring into Josh's eyes, then Fargo's. He said something, only a few clipped sounds coming from the back of his throat, making a sweeping motion with his right hand.

"There ain't no way to tell him we don't understand," Josh said over his shoulder.

In the following silence Fargo noticed a distant sound coming from the center of the village . . . it could have been women crying or wailing. "About all we can do is get close enough so I can give 'em these beads an' the knife," he said. "If they aimed to kill us, they'd have done it by now. Let's paddle up to the bank. I'll get out an' hand the tall one what we're offerin'. Keep your rifle low, but handy. Don't start shooting unless somethin' goes wrong."

Josh paddled a few more strokes, sending the canoe straight for shore. More Indians approached the riverbank, coming from all over the village to stare at the new arrivals. Most of them were staring at Josh, pointing to him.

Where water was barely a foot deep, Fargo swung a leg over the side of the canoe and stepped out, extending his gifts in an outstretched hand while trying to get his balance in river mud and sand. He walked toward the Apache leader, whispering to himself until he stood on dry land.

"*Hi, hites. Nodemah.*"

The Apache looked at Fargo's beads. He made a grunting noise and reached for the knife, snatching it from Fargo's palm as if he feared it might be taken away. He examined the blade carefully, touching the edge with his fingers, then the tip. His gaze went to Josh immediately thereafter as though he was curious about the color of Josh's skin.

Fargo turned to a younger Indian standing beside him. He held out a string of yellow beads. The Apache seemed uncertain, but after a sideways glance at his leader, he reached for the beads very slowly and accepted them, saying nothing.

Fargo offered the red beads to another Apache. "*Nodemah*," he said. The Indian took them cautiously, keeping his eyes on Fargo.

The leader spoke to Fargo then, and no single word was distinguishable from any other. His obsidian eyes were fixed on Fargo and he felt sure he was waiting some sort of answer to a question. Again, his eyes flickered to Josh where they remained for several seconds.

"We can't speak in your tongue." As he spoke, he noticed several of the men standing around him had tiny red bumps on their faces and upper bodies. Some had become open sores oozing puss. He took a second, closer look at one of the young men covered by sores and he knew at once what it was.

Fargo spoke to Josh without turning around. "Looks like some of 'em have got smallpox. Take a look at the red bumps on their faces." He and Josh had both survived smallpox epidemics sweeping through the South, back in the late thirties.

Josh answered very softly. "That do appear to be what it is they's got, Skye."

The tall Apache spoke once more, and as before, Fargo could not recognize a word. The Indian was looking at Josh when he spoke.

"We don't understand," Fargo explained, certain now that the Indian had no idea what he was saying. He pointed to the river behind him, indicating that he and Josh meant to travel upstream. "We may be able to find somebody who can speak your language for us in a few days. Meantime, we leave you in peace."

As Fargo was turning for the canoe, the Apache spoke sharply to an Indian standing behind him. The younger boy took off at a run into the heart of the village, causing Fargo to stop and ponder why he'd been sent away.

Josh was wondering, too. "Maybe they's got somebody who can talk English. Could be that's why one of 'em ran off just now. Let's wait an' see if he comes back. Maybe it's that girl you been daydreamin' about."

Fargo noticed the Apache spokesman examining his knife again with a slight frown on his face, turning it over in his hands, letting sunlight reflect off its surface as though he'd never seen a metal object before.

A commotion in the village caused Fargo to glance that way as voices ended a moment of silence. Then he saw a sight that made him take a deep breath . . . every muscle in his body tensed. A man was being led toward the river by a rope tied to a collar around his neck, pulled by two young Apache men. The man wearing the rope was starved beyond belief, completely naked other than the leather collar around his neck, little more than a skeleton with sun-darkened skin stretched over his bones. He staggered as the rope was being pulled and almost fell, struggling to remain on his feet while answering the pull on his rope with bony fingers holding his collar away from his throat to keep from strangling. Even from a distance it was easy to see he was not an Indian, and it was clear he was a prisoner here. His features were so badly sunken it was hard to tell what his face might have looked like otherwise.

The Apaches pulled their starved prisoner down to the river and when they arrived, the others stood aside. Fargo gave Josh a quick backward glance, then he turned to the prisoner, looking for some sort of explanation.

The man's dark green eyes looked dull. He stared at Fargo for a moment, swaying drunkenly to stay on his feet, touching his bony rib cage with trembling fingers. He had dark purple bruises over most of his body and several old cuts that had begun to heal over with scabs. "Are you here to help?" a thin, weak voice asked, looking past Fargo to Josh.

"We are," Fargo replied softly, barely able to speak after a closer examination of the prisoner's tragic physical condition. "Why have they got that rope around your neck?"

Tears brimmed in his eyelids now. "They made me a slave of sorts. There was a misunderstanding. They believe my followers and I brought a curse to their people. Many of them are dying from smallpox and they believe we are the cause of it, that their gods have turned against them because they listened to us."

"Your followers?" Fargo asked without thinking. "Who are you? And what are you doin' here in the first place?"

"My name," he began, "is Augustine Huerta. I am Franciscan, a Catholic priest. We came here last year to build a mission in the wilderness to teach Christian principles to these people, the Mimbres Apache tribe. We began building our church. My stonemasons did splendid work and we established peaceful relations with the Apaches. Until the terrible sickness began. Some of them died last fall. During the winter it only grew worse. The disease has spread to neighboring tribes, the Comonses and Osage. They seem to have no natural ability to survive smallpox and now they are dying at an alarming rate. This spring, Chief Mangas Coloradas came with a hundred warriors. They killed my Franciscan brothers in the most brutal fashion imaginable, taking me prisoner, making me a slave. They starved me, as you can see, and unless the epidemic ends soon, they will kill me. They believe we brought some evil spirit among their people. Smallpox was apparently unknown to them until we arrived. More are dying every day . . ."

"You're Father Augustine," Fargo said. "One of your priests, a fellow by the name of Father Olivares, is behind us, lookin' for you and a mission called Santa Fe. He was sent here from San Antonio to bring you seeds and supplies, only he got robbed by a couple of soldiers when war with Mexico broke out down in Texas. The priest who was with him was killed. Father Olivares is only a few hours from here, travelin' by cart, headed this way."

"They will kill him when they see his cleric's robes. They believe we are something evil. They are keeping me alive so they can torture me, believing it may appease their gods."

Josh spoke quietly from the canoe's prow. "Only way to stop smallpox is separate them that's got it from them that ain't, an' to burn their clothes an' bedding. How come you ain't told 'em that?"

"They no longer listen to anything I say, believing I am an evil spirit."

Suddenly, the Apache chief spoke, pointing to the canoe, at Josh. "*To-oh Tivo. Tuh-yah po-haw-cut.*"

Fargo looked to Father Augustine for an explanation.

"He asks if he is a medicine man from some unknown tribe. In Apache religion they speak of black medicine men who returned from the dead in olden days. The chief is not sure if they should be afraid of him, of his spiritual medicine. He asks if the black man can be a messenger god from the spirit world below ground. These are very superstitious people. They act like they are somewhat afraid of him, of the color of his skin and his tremendous size."

Fargo was about to ask the priest to explain, when Josh spoke softly behind him. "Let 'em think whatever they want, Skye, so long as they don't start shootin' arrows at us."

All eyes were on Josh as he talked and Fargo wondered if the deep sound of his voice added to the Indians' fear of him. "Get out of the canoe, Josh, so they can see you're a man. Don't do anything to frighten 'em . . . just walk up here beside me so they can see you're made of flesh an' bone."

Josh stepped slowly out of the canoe with his rifle in his hands. "I ain't comin' without these guns, Skye, no matter what you say. Don't none of 'em look all that friendly."

When Josh stood his full height, several Apache men backed away from the river's edge. The chief remained where he was as Josh walked out of the river. But when Josh stopped alongside Fargo, the chief looked up at Josh, being as he was a full head taller than the Indian, and for the first time Fargo noticed a subtle change in the chief's flat expression. He looked at the rifle Josh carried; then he spoke to Father Augustine.

"*To-oh Tivo tuh-yah po-haw-cut te-bit-se,*" he said. "*Pe-ie ein mah-ri eh ah-hit-to.*"

"The chief says this giant is surely the medicine man who comes back from the dead," Augustine explained. "He asks about the gun. He calls it a medicine rod or stick, and he has heard from other tribes of a medicine rod that makes a big noise and kills its enemies. He also says to tell the giant they want peace with him. They have never seen a black man before, nor a man of his size. To them, he is a medicine man sent from the spirit world and I'm afraid almost nothing will change their minds."

"Suits the hell outa me," Josh muttered. "They won't be as likely to try an' kill us then."

Fargo noticed the chief was still glancing warily at Josh's rifle. "In that case, we'll make the best of it," he said. He spoke to Father Augustine. "Tell them Josh is like a medicine man, a doctor, an' if they'll listen, he can show 'em how to end their smallpox, if they'll do exactly like he says. We'll have 'em move the ones with pox to a separate place an' burn all the clothing. The ones with red spots have to stay off to themselves for several weeks."

"It's the way they done it in New Orleans," Josh remembered aloud. "Tell 'em we can stop it from spreadin' if they'll listen an' do what we say."

Augustine turned to the chief. He began speaking Apache and to Fargo, it sounded no differently than when it was spoken by the Indians. But even while the naked priest was talking, most every Apache watched Josh closely.

"Nearly makes me wanna laugh," Josh whispered. "Anybody who thinks I'm an Injun medicine man has gotta be a bit on the crazy side. Appears they never heard of no black slaves. Only reason I'm a free man now is I got papers from the man who owned my pappy."

As soon as Augustine finished his explanation, the chief pointed to Josh's rifle.

"*Pe-ie. Nah-ich-ka.*"

Augustine spoke softly. "He wants to hear the medicine rod make a loud noise. I'm sure it will frighten them and I pray you won't shoot anyone during the demonstration."

Josh adopted a serious look. "Tell the chief I'm gonna fire it up at the sky, to kill the evil spirits causin' them to die of smallpox. Only remind him, they'll have to do what we say to get rid of it."

Augustine nodded. "I understand. These Mimbres are difficult to turn aside from their primitive beliefs." He turned to the chief and spoke rapidly in the Apaches' tongue.

The moment Augustine fell silent, Josh aimed the muzzle of his Whitney skyward and drew the hammer back. A few Indians standing close backed away; however the chief stood perfectly still watching Josh's every movement.

To put on a better show, Josh threw back his head and let out a yell. "Hallelujah!"

When he pulled the trigger, the Whitney's explosion sent Indians running in every direction. Only the chief stood where he was without flinching, looking up at the sky as though he expected to see something fall from it. As the thunderous noise echoed and faded away, the chief closed the palm of his right hand over his heart and said, "*Su-vate.*"

"He believes you now," Father Augustine said.

14

Their campsite in an oak grove beside the river was quiet, still at dawn's first light. Across the river wood ducks hunted shallows for small fish, their white-banded bodies radiant even in pale skies brightening with daybreak. A gray crane stalked through strands of bulrushes searching for prey and for a moment, Fargo sat, enjoying the river's peace, its beauty. They were camped less than two miles upstream from the Apache village, and as he awakened fully his mind drifted back to the sick members of the tribe.

So many of them will die, he thought. He wondered if their truce with their chief would last if too many more of his people succumbed to smallpox. A part of the trade they made was to take Father Augustine with them. As they paddled upstream last night they passed three more feeder creeks in the darkness, all bearing evidence of beaver activity along their thickly wooded banks. But would the chief allow a fur trapper to stay in his territorial lands when scores of his people died? If the sickness continued to spread? The chief believed in Josh's magic, but of course there was no magic, only a quarantine Fargo doubted the Apaches understood and a pinch of gunpowder in a gunshot.

"It's like gamblin'," he told himself softly. "You take the best odds an' play 'em out to the end. I'm headed back to El Paso, anyway, to pick up my horses and head for the mountains." The Indians' belief in Josh's magical powers might be enough to hold them off him through most of the winter . . . unless the quarantine failed.

Josh sat up in his bedroll. "Heard you talkin' to yourself, Skye."

"Just wonderin' out loud if they'll let you stay here."

"No need wonderin'. I can move farther west up the river if things don't work out. This is the best beaver country I ever did see an' I ain't gonna be inclined to give up an' leave it on account of some sick Injuns. I move west, maybe it gets better."

Augustine rolled out of a blanket borrowed from Josh. "I've been listening to what you were saying," he said sleepily. He yawned. "I can assure you the Apaches are unusually susceptible to death from smallpox. They die at an alarming rate as though they somehow lack the capacity to recover from it. Their children are the most likely to die in its early stages, when fever is the most common evidence they have contracted it. These people have little understanding of disease, almost as if they never experience it. I believe this is why they have blamed me and my brother Franciscans for what is happening. Until we came here, smallpox was apparently unknown to them, a most unfortunate coincidence for the furtherance of our mission to teach them Christianity."

Josh gave the river a lingering look. "Can't exactly say it's our fault, Father Augustine, that they ain't got whatever it takes to get over it." He watched ducks swim against the river's current for a moment. "Best I remember, the pox takes a spell to stop on its own."

Augustine nodded. "We had outbreaks in Mexico City several years ago. I wish I could remember more of what happened. The bishop sent us to minister to the sick and dying in poorer parts of the city where the illness seemed worst. I gave last rites to so many. However, the disease seemed to run its course and then it stopped. Physicians dealt with all forms of treatment. We were there to minister to their souls . . ."

Fargo looked downstream, toward the village. "We'll know in a few weeks, I reckon. Till then, we'll scout for beaver dams an' a place where Josh can build a shelter for the winter. Stop by the village every now an' then to see if the pox has stopped spreadin'. I don't see much else we can do."

"Word will spread to other Apache bands of Mr. Brooks's magic and we should expect them to come, seeking his help. If you intend to remain in Apache lands this winter you'll be asked to help them as well. Your reputation as a medicine man will soon reach the other bands."

Josh got up slowly, stretching, watching the sunrise. "Got no objections to helpin' them others," he said quietly, thoughtfully, "so long as it don't interfere with trappin' beaver. If bein' an Apache medicine man includes gettin' all the beaver pelts I want, then I'll make as much magic as I can . . . till the gunpowder runs out."

Fargo gave it little thought. As soon as he'd helped Josh get his shelter erected, he'd be paddling back toward El Paso.

15

They were summoned by a horseback messenger who spoke to Augustine rapidly, shouting and pointing to the east as though something of importance was taking place. Fargo stopped what he was doing to listen carefully to what the Indian said, although in the few days they'd been camped in Apache territory he had only learned a few simple words from both priests, Father Augustine and Father Olivares. When Father Augustine told them what the messenger wanted, he'd turned to Josh and told him to gather up their guns. A large party of Comanche warriors had been sighted entering Apache lands and the Apache chief, whose name meant Bull Bear, expected a fight, an attack on their village, asking that Josh return as quickly as possible to perform some sort of magic that would allow his weakened people to defend themselves. As much as Fargo wanted no part of a war, he knew he couldn't turn his back on them.

"He don't understand," Josh had said, as they shoved their canoe into the river, leaving Father Olivares behind. "Only magic we've got is havin' a good aim an' a steady pair of hands with a rifle."

"Maybe we can scare 'em off," Fargo suggested,

"shootin' up in the air, or wingin' one or two. Hadn't bargained on gettin' no Indian war, but if you aim to stay, as your guide I think we'd better do what we can to help these people."

They paddled down to the village in a scant quarter hour with the current pushing them, watched closely by the messenger who rode along the riverbank. Passing the quarantined group, Fargo noted a few tents had been erected, a dozen or more. And as their canoe drifted by, he saw a young boy standing near a leafless oak tree beside the river, staring at them as they rowed past. His upper body and face were covered with red pockmarks and his skin appeared to be stretched across his rib cage. While he carried a bow and a sling of arrows he didn't appear to be in any fighting condition if his village came under attack.

"Some of 'em's getting worse," Josh observed, pausing with his paddle raised above the water. Between two trees, a row of corpses lay covered in buffalo skins. "I see more dead bodies over yonder. Damned if it don't seem all of 'em's gonna die from it afore it's done."

Fargo steered around a bend where the river swept past Bull Bear's camp. He gave the boy a final glance and turned his attention downstream when he saw men on horses gathered along the bank. Fifty or sixty Apache warriors sat on their ponies, carrying weapons and crude buffalohide shields. He noticed their faces were painted—streaks of yellow and red and white drawn across their cheeks below their eyes. Even their ponies were painted, flanks sporting red handprints or designs, feathers tied into their manes and tails.

"Hell of a sight, ain't it?" Josh asked. "You ain't gotta know nothin' 'bout Injuns to know they's ready to put up one hell of a fight with somebody, an' we've got ourselves square in the middle. I came up this river to get away from trouble an' live peaceful. Appears I guessed wrong. They look mighty ferocious painted up like that."

Augustine said, "Tribal warfare is as old as time between them and most neighboring tribes. They see it as necessary, to protect their territory and belongings. We couldn't persuade them otherwise in the short time we were here."

Fargo saw Chief Mangas sitting on a pinto pony near the water's edge. His face bore streaks of black and yellow paint below his eyes. He watched the canoe approach without moving, like a statue carved from copper-colored stone wearing a headdress of eagle feathers trailing off his pony's flank. In full regalia he was a fearsome figure. Fargo had fought his share of men over a lifetime and he judged the chief would be a wily adversary, quick, deadly if he had an advantage. "Wish we wasn't expected to lend a hand," he said, thinking out loud as they turned for shore, "but maybe a few gunshots will turn them Comanches back before real trouble starts. The others we saw back down the river took off soon as we dropped that pair clubbin' those women. Maybe it was the noise scared 'em. If we're lucky it'll be that easy this time . . ."

Josh stepped out of the canoe and pulled it ashore, balancing his rifle in one hand. Mangas watched Josh's every move carefully, as did all the other Apaches gathered around him. Fargo got out and helped Father Augustine to the bank, cradling his own rifle in the crook of an arm.

Augustine approached the chief and began to speak.

For some time Mangas said nothing, until the priest fell silent.

"*Nah-taih sic ba-ton. To-ho-ba-ka ma-way-kin.*"

"He says the Comanches are coming, that there are many and they are few because of the illness. He asks you to use your magic to help them," Augustine explained, speaking to Josh.

Josh looked over to Fargo, and when Fargo nodded Josh spoke to the chief. "Tell him we'll help. Ask him to show us where he figures they'll be comin' from, so me an' Skye can find a spot to shoot. Tell him to let us use our magic before he sends his men off to fight. We'll see if we can scare 'em off with a dose of lead an' gunpowder."

Augustine translated for Mangas, halting now and then when he wasn't sure of a word. Mangas Coloradas's eyes went from the priest to Josh, flickering occasionally to the rifle or Josh's belted pistol or the long knife sheathed at his waist.

The chief spoke, pointing to the northeast.

"He will show us the direction from which they will come and he warns they are very close now. He also wonders if your magic will be powerful enough to stop them because there are so many of the Comanche warriors . . . more than a hundred, his scouts tell him."

Josh stared up at the chief. "You can say he ain't got all that much to worry 'bout. Me an' Skye been up against long odds before. Won't be our first one-sided fight. Me an' Skye's had our share of experience evenin' things up."

A wooded slope ran down to a winding creek flowing through a shallow valley. Fall leaves added their colors to dry grasses blanketing every hillside. All was quiet. A stirring rustled leaves when breaths of wind swept along the valley floor. Josh and Fargo stood behind thick oak trunks high on a hilltop overlooking the valley. Along ridges on either side of them, Apache men hid their ponies just below the horizon, out of sight from below.

Fargo studied every movement, every swirl of air turning leaves or bending branches along the stream. An hour passed silently. Up and down the lines of Apache warriors, occasionally a pony stamped a hoof or pawed the ground as though the animals sensed a presence close by, the nearness of danger. Chief Mangas Coloradas sent scouts across the valley when they first arrived and as yet, the scouts had not returned.

Augustine spoke softly from his hiding place behind a tree. "Mangas sent messengers to another tribe, asking for help. The Apache tribes are widely scattered this fall preparing for winter and he doesn't expect help to arrive in time. This is why he asked you to come. He doesn't trust his own spirit medicine any longer. He believes Mr. Brooks has the counsel of Tutoco, their Great Spirit."

Josh chuckled mirthlessly. "All I's got is a Whitney rifle an' good eyes, Father. Don't reckon there's no need to tell him that just now. Me an' Skye will let our rifles do the talkin'."

Fargo studied a wooded slope across the valley. "They can call it spirit medicine or whatever they want," he said quietly. "Let's just hope too many of 'em don't rush us all at once, so we'll have time to reload . . ." He was interrupted when a rider galloped over a distant ridge; then another horseman came right on his heels. "The scouts are comin' back," he muttered, "an' it looks like they saw somethin', ridin' hard as they are." He felt his hands grow damp around his rifle stock. "I 'spect it won't be long before the shootin' starts."

Josh shouldered his Whitney, peering through its sights for a moment. "Let 'em come," he whispered savagely, as muscles hardened in his cheeks. "They come lookin' for a fight. We'll give 'em plenty."

A distant cry echoed across the valley as the scouts pushed their ponies down to the stream. Splashing across, they swung in the direction of Chief Mangas, drumming their heels into their ponies' sides.

Suddenly the far side of the valley came alive with swarms of mounted Indians. Multicolored ponies swept over the crests of hills, darting between trees, galloping full speed down every slope and ravine toward the bottom of the valley. Yipping cries like coyote calls accompanied the charge. Comanche warriors, their twin braids of black hair bobbing up and down with their ponies' gait, clung to the backs of their horses as the animals dodged trees and rocks at a breakneck run to reach the stream. Fargo felt his chest tighten.

A group of Comanches started upslope after the pair of Apache scouts. Josh spoke to Fargo over his shoulder as screams from the valley grew louder. "I'll take the bastard on that white pony, Skye," he said, swinging his sights to the left where a shouting warrior leaned over the neck of a bounding white horse with a bow and arrow in his hands.

Fargo put his sights on a rider aboard a calico dun, moving the notch so his muzzle sight rested on the warrior's chest. He thumbed back the Henry's hammer and waited, holding his breath. It would be a tricky shot, but not impossible if he allowed for just the right amount of drop to account for distance. He waited a moment longer, making sure, listening to the cries swelling down below and the drumming of pony hooves moving steadily closer.

The crack of a rifle made him flinch . . . he hadn't expected Josh to take a shot at this range. A puff of cottony smoke boiled away from Josh's gun barrel and in the same instant, a sharp cry arose from the slope.

The Comanche riding the white pony was torn from the back of his horse as though he'd run into some invisible barrier. He flew backward, tossing his bow and arrow into the air to clutch his chest, tumbling ball-like off the rump of his pony, spinning for a moment in midair before he fell to the grass and disappeared.

Fargo corrected his aim slightly and nudged the Henry's trigger as gently as he knew how. The butt plate slammed into his shoulder as gunpowder exploded. The roar of the gun hurt his ears. A breath of smoke spat from the muzzle just fractions of a second after the recoil ended. He blinked, waiting for the gunsmoke in front of his eyes to clear.

The Indian perched on the spotted dun's withers floated off to one side, kicking and screaming, pawing his stomach as the force of impact carried him away. He fell hard on his back, skidding through tangles of deep grass—his pony swerved and broke stride to change directions, forcing another mounted Indian to swing wide to avoid a riderless horse.

Comanches charging toward the trees were looking over their shoulder following the pair of gunshots. One slowed his horse and stopped, staring back at his downed companions like he couldn't quite believe what he had seen. Others halted their ponies to look backward and for a moment, their charge was broken just long enough for Josh and Fargo to reload.

Before Fargo could take aim again, Josh's rifle thundered. A Comanche warrior yelped, tumbling off his sorrel pony just as the winded little horse bounded to a stop near a patch of blood-stained grass where the first warrior had fallen. All but one of the Comanches halted there . . . a single Indian riding a sleek black pony continued at a hard gallop toward the trees with an arrow fitted to his bowstring.

Fargo turned the muzzle of his rifle and took careful aim. In a matter of seconds he squeezed the trigger . . . fate caused the pony to stumble, and his shot went high, whining harmlessly over the warrior's head.

Josh swung around the tree trunk with his Paterson aimed up at the Comanche's face. The crack of igniting gunpowder drowned out the drumming of hooves. The Indian's right cheek puckered where Josh's ball stuck him and his head twisted violently, turning him backward amid the snap of splintering bone. The black pony snorted and lunged past the tree as the Comanche slid off its back and fell, landing disjointedly on his belly a few feet away from Josh.

Confusion and obvious fear ran through the Comanches coming upslope when they heard guns and saw warriors falling. They reined their ponies to a halt all across the valley to look up at the spot where Fargo and Josh were shooting. Their war cries ended and for a moment things were still, silent as more than a hundred Indians abruptly halted their charge.

The coppery scent of blood drifted past the tree where Fargo stood, and he wrinkled his nose, hurrying to reload his rifle. A pony snorted somewhere behind him when it too caught the smell of fresh blood.

Unexpectedly, Josh slipped off his sleeveless cotton shirt and stuck his pistol in his belt, then he walked away from the oak tree toward the warrior he shot. Standing out in plain sight of Indians downslope, he bent down and lifted the Comanche in his arms. Fargo's lips formed to shout a warning, when Josh did the strangest thing of all.

Hoisting the dead warrior above his head, thick muscles rippling in his arms and chest while blood from the Indian's wound dribbled over his face and body, Josh threw back his head and bellowed, "Hallelujah!" at the top of his lungs. Then he gave a mighty heave and threw the body as far as he could downhill.

The corpse flew a dozen feet and landed with a thump where it began rolling through matted grass. It rolled a few feet more before it finally came to a halt.

Josh drew his pistol, glaring down into the valley. He gave another roar, "Hallelujah!" and fired the Paterson over his head.

Perhaps it was the unfamiliar color of his skin, along with his booming voice and being witness to gunshots killing members of their tribe that made the Comanches back away. A few at a time, then in groups, mounted warriors turned away from Josh and began a slow retreat toward the valley floor.

16

At the village, news of the Apache victory had already reached scores of women and children and older men—laughter came from a number of groups gathered by the river near the canoe. But when the Indians saw Josh and Fargo enter a clearing around the village, silence spread quickly. Then a half-dozen women emerged from one of the tents carrying armloads of buffalo robes, clay pots and curiously shaped fans made from eagle feathers. The women came toward them, bowing their heads meekly, and before Fargo reached them their gifts were placed on the ground blocking Fargo's path to the canoe.

An older woman spoke to Augustine, speaking in a soft voice while looking at the ground.

"The woman is one of Chief Mangas's wives," Augustine said. "Like many of the most powerful Apaches in his tribe, he has several wives. It is Chief Mangas's wish that offerings of buffalo skins and food be given to you and Mr. Brooks. They believe in the power of his magic, his spirit medicine, and they have seen proof his spirit medicine was strong enough to defeat their worst enemies, the Nah-taih."

"We don't need no more buffalo robes," Josh began.

Augustine raised a hand. "They will be offended if you do not accept their offering, Mr. Brooks. They are unable to understand why anyone would do something in their behalf without expecting something in return. My advice to you is to take the robes and food. It will be a long, cold winter and the robes will be valuable. The cooking pots contain a mixture of acorn bread, to which they add wild berries and nuts. It is actually quite tasty, and as I said before, Mangas will be offended if you refuse them. If you wish to trap beaver here, I would advise you to take them."

"We'll take 'em along," Fargo said quietly. "An' tell the chief we're grateful, only we ain't gonna take no part of any more wars between Comanches an' his tribe. Josh came here to live peaceful trappin' beaver, an' that's the way he aims to spend the winter here. We ain't soldiers."

Augustine nodded as though he understood. "The only problem with your peaceful intentions is that they now believe Mr. Brooks was sent to help them by their spirit ancestors. War is as much a part of their lives as gathering food. Should you refuse to help them in the future, Chief Mangas may see it as some form of disfavor from their spirits." He glanced in the direction of a tent where the tribal holy man stood watching them, arms folded across his chest. "And you have an enemy among them now. Their medicine man will look for any excuse to discredit you with his chief in order to enhance his position within the tribe. I understand you wish to live peacefully among these people, Mr. Brooks, however, as you have already seen today, they have a very limited view of peaceful relations with their neighbors."

"We didn't paddle all the way up this river to get

involved in no Injun wars," Josh argued, scowling. "I'm in the fur-trappin' business an' by God, that's the way I intend to stay. There's a thousand other creeks leadin' into this river. I'll move farther west if they won't let me live here peaceful. In a day or so, Skye is goin' back down to El Paso in the canoe to fetch his horses. I'll take my skins to market on a raft made of logs, so it'll just be me an' them two priests here this winter. We ain't interested in doin' no more fightin'. I'll go farther north if I have to."

Augustine looked worried. "I'm afraid going north won't be the direction to travel, Mr. Brooks. North of Apache territory lies the land of the northern Comanches and the Osages. If any tribe of western Indians is more warlike than the Apaches, it will be any one of the five Comanche bands or the Osages. While I have no personal knowledge of their habits, we have heard reports that they are even more brutal and unreasoning than their Apache enemies."

Josh looked at Fargo. "I made up my mind to leave that damn Mississip' on account of all the trouble. Don't seem we've found what I was hopin' for here." He fingered his rifle. "It ain't that I'm against killin' another man, Skye. You've seen me do it. But I had it figured I'd find some empty land out here where I had a chance to make a livin' without spillin' any more blood. I was aimin' to live quiet the rest of my days without no more dead men to add to a tally book."

Fargo watched the Apache women walk away from the piles of gifts. "About all we can do is ask Father Augustine to explain it to 'em as plain as he can. We didn't come here to fight, just to trade for the right to run your traps. If the chief can't be made to understand, then we'll break camp an' go somewheres else.

I'm of the same mind on it as you . . . we done about all the killin' any man oughta. I've got a horse herd waitin' for me back in El Paso an' they need to be headed toward Colorado Territory. If livin' peaceful don't suit Chief Bull Bear, then you'll move on an' take your chances with those Comanches and Osages."

As they were talking, a lathered pony galloped from a grove of trees north of the village bearing a rider clad in deerskin leggings. He jerked his pony to a bounding halt near the river and began shouting to some of the older men standing around the canoe.

"What's goin' on?" Josh asked, casting a worried look in Augustine's direction.

The priest's face darkened. "I'm afraid there is more bad news, gentlemen. The rider is a messenger from Chief Bull Bear's tribe. Another battle has taken place. While Bull Bear and his hunters were out gathering buffalo meat for the winter, the village was attacked by another Comanche band. The village was not prepared for war with their fighting men off on buffalo hunts. A terrible toll has been exacted against Bull Bear's people." He fell silent long enough to listen to more of what the rider was saying. "The messenger says women and children were killed by the Nah-taih, and their heads were . . . cut off. The heads were put in clay cooking pots as a declaration of all-out war between the Nah-taih and the Apaches. I fear the peace you were hoping for is quite impossible now. Bull Bear and Mangas will call a council. A terrible Indian war is sure to follow, gentlemen. This territory will become a battleground and nothing short of a miracle can prevent it. The Apaches will unite to fight off a Comanche incursion and to seek revenge for what has happened to Mangas's tribe."

Fargo immediately thought about Chokole. "I hope she escaped somehow . . ." he drifted.

Augustine didn't appear to be listening, paying closer attention to what the messenger from Bull Bear's band was saying to Apaches gathered around him. "He says the slaughter was by far the worst in recent memory, since trouble began between the two tribes."

"Maybe it's time we both pulled out of here," Fargo said to Josh. "Fur trappin' might not be so good this winter, and a man could lose his life, caught in the middle of a Comanche an' Apache war."

17

Even Fargo, who was usually calm in the face of any kind of trouble, had grown edgy as two days passed. Since their fight with the Comanches they spent long hours finishing a lean-to above the fork where the stream joined the Rio Grande, aided by Father Olivares and Father Augustine. A crude shelter of trimmed tree trunks and branches provided a break from growing winds as fall slowly gave way to the first signs of winter. Nights grew colder. During the day sunlight warmed forested hills around them, but when darkness came a deepening chill swept down from the north as winds shifted with a change of seasons. No word had come from the Apache village since Josh and Fargo and Father Augustine returned.

"Seems like your mind is someplace else," Josh said. A smoldering fire burned near the front of the lean-to, causing Josh's eyes to burn when wind swirled smoke near his face. "We's in the heart of good beaver country an' you don't act like you give a damn 'bout it. This is where you was supposed to take me."

"I'm leavin' for El Paso in a day or two, soon as we finish this lean-to. I understand why you decided to stay, along with the priests, but I've got business elsewhere."

They heard the creak of cart wheels coming through a wooded ravine to the west. Olivares and Augustine were out gathering limbs for the roof all morning and as noon approached, Fargo had begun to worry some. "I ain't forgot why we came, Josh. You spent too many years dreamin' about this to let an Indian war take your mind off business."

Josh grunted, watching the two priests approach, leading the bay pulling its loaded cart. "This Injun war got me a touch on the jumpy side, too. If those two bunches start fightin' it could get mighty dangerous workin' traps up some of these creeks should we get caught between 'em. Let them do the fightin' an' I'll take my profits back to New Orleans without no extra holes in my skin."

"Father Augustine says Bull Bear will ask for your help if the Comanches come again. They believe you've got supernatural powers."

Josh shrugged and went back to tying a bundle of limbs to a roof support with a piece of twine. "All I's got is good aim," he said quietly.

The priests came along the bottom of the draw and Fargo took note that they both looked worried. Before the cart rolled to a halt Augustine began to speak, pointing over his shoulder.

"We've been followed," he said, looking up the ravine they had traveled. "About a hundred mounted Indians keeping to the woods behind us. They were letting us know they were there, making no real attempt to hide themselves. I'm not quite sure what to make of their behavior."

Josh moved quickly to his guns, sticking the Paterson in the waistband of his pants before Fargo made it to his rifle.

"How far back is they?" Josh asked, stepping over to a tree trunk behind the lean-to while peering up the ravine.

Father Olivares said breathlessly, "They are very close, only a few hundred *varas*. I believe they are Apaches. I'm very sure of it."

Fargo checked his Henry before he put his pistol in his pants, squinting into the sun's glare to see if any horsemen came from the draw. The past days of quiet had given him a false sense of security. "If they're Apaches they shouldn't give us any trouble," he said, as much to reassure himself as to convince anyone else.

Then he saw them, counting seven riders as they emerged from a line of trees and brush choking the floor of the ravine. He held his breath a moment, looking for signs of aggression or any weapons held in a threatening way.

"They's Apaches," Josh observed, "only don't none of 'em look like Mangas's bunch. Don't recognize no faces, 'cept for maybe one. Look at the one ridin' way back, Skye. It's a woman, if she's not one of them girls who's got you so moonstruck, she oughta be."

He recognized Chokole at once. Another girl rode beside her on a dappled mare. The women stayed back while all five warriors rode slowly toward their camp beside the river. The men carried bows, but no arrows were fitted to the strings.

The Indian riding in front was a curious figure, a young man with fierce black eyes and rippling muscles underneath his copper skin. He had a pair of scars running down one cheek as though he had been cut severely with a knife some time in the past. His pony was a piebald stallion prancing under the restraint of a jaw rein.

"Their leader, the one riding the spotted horse, that is Chief Bull Bear," Augustine said in a hushed voice. "He is said to be very unpredictable. The girl who came to the mission is there on a black pony, the one named Chokole, who eagerly learned English from us until . . . until the epidemic began."

Bull Bear stopped his pony near the back of the priests' cart. His cold stare lingered on Josh a moment.

"*To-oh Tivo po-haw-cut Tatoco*," he said, addressing Josh as though he understood.

Augustine translated. "He is asking if you are the medicine man sent by the Great Spirit."

Josh looked at the priest. "What the hell do I say? I'm no medicine man."

Augustine appeared thoughtful. "I suppose he was told what the two of you did to help Chief Mangas against the Nah-taih. In their eyes, you have strong medicine because your guns killed so many of their enemies in ways they do not understand."

"You can say I'm the same one who helped Mangas's people, only you'd best explain we ain't interested in doin' no more fightin' for nobody."

Augustine began speaking Apache. Father Olivares cowered at the front of his cart as though he expected arrows to fly at any moment. While Augustine was talking, Fargo let his eyes drift back to the girl.

She wore a short deerskin dress pulled high on her thighs by the way she clung to her pony's back with her legs. Her black hair fell below her shoulders, surrounding the most unusual face he had ever seen. Her cheekbones were so high and broad as to give the impression she was smiling, however her mouth was drawn in a thin line and there was no friendliness in her eyes. She stared at Fargo, then she looked away while Augustine continued to talk. Fargo recalled their wonderful moment at the creek and something stirred in his loins.

Bull Bear seemed displeased by what the priest said. He spoke sharply, pointing to the river, then to Josh, making a number of small gestures with one hand. His eyes passed over Fargo quickly. When he fell silent it was clear by the expression on Augustine's face there was bad news.

"Bull Bear is angry, demanding to know why you helped his brothers and now you say you will not use your magic to help his people against the Nah-taih. He is asking for your blessing, I think, rather than help from your guns. These people believe in magic and if they think you have given them some sort of magical powers in battle by asking the Great Spirit to intervene, they will be victorious. He has never seen a man with black skin before and attributes your color to Apache legend, that a dark messenger from the spirit world belowground will come to save them from being driven from their ancestral lands by enemies. He wants to know if Mr. Fargo is also a medicine man."

Josh glanced over to Fargo. "I suppose I can tell him I'll do a little prayin' for him, but I sure as hell don't want no part of this brewin' an' neither do you. As to the part about Skye, you can say he's got as much magic as me."

"We want to avoid any more fightin' if we can," Fargo said. "Have Augustine tell Bull Bear you'll use all your influence with the Great Spirit, but that we're done fightin' for now. Have him say we came to trap beaver, an' that if they'll leave you alone to run your trap lines you'll cook up as much magic as you can to help 'em."

Josh turned to the priest. "Tell him exactly what Skye just told me, that I'll pray to whatever spirits they want for his victory. Explain that we're after beaver skins, an' if they'll leave me be to run traps up these creeks this winter I'll give 'em more knives like the one he's got an' strings of beads. I'll talk to them spirits an' ask for an Apache victory over his enemies."

The priest appeared uncertain before he began a translation of what was said. While he was talking, Fargo rested his Henry against his leg to watch the girl again, without making himself too obvious about it.

Chokole was looking at him, too, but when she felt his eyes she looked away. The girl seated on the gray pony beside her said something quietly, before she too looked askance.

He marveled at the smoothness of her skin, rounded places underneath her dress, the shape of her legs. She was every bit as beautiful as he remembered . . . perhaps even more so when he examined her features more closely.

When Augustine finished talking there was a moment of uneasy silence. Chief Bull Bear stared at Josh, then at Fargo, all but ignoring the two priests.

"He wasn't happy with your answer," Augustine whispered. "I fear we may have fallen into disfavor with him now."

Josh sensed the same uneasiness between him and the chief. He placed his rifle against a wall of the lean-to and took a pinch of gunpowder from his ammunition pouch. Bull Bear watched him closely, suspicion on his face. Josh approached the fire and held his arms in the air.

Josh's booming voice echoed from trees surrounding the camp when he cried, "Hallelujah!" He swept his palms back and forth over the fire twice, then a ball of flame and smoke erupted from the bed of coals, accompanied by a loud bang.

The Indians' ponies snorted and tried to whirl away from the unexpected sound. The girl beside Chokole lost her balance and fell to the earth when her gray mare bolted to escape the noise. Chief Bull Bear's pony, being closest to the explosion, reared on its hind legs and attempted to run off until he brought it under control with a sharp jerk on its rein.

A moment was required for the Indians to settle their horses as the cloud of gunsmoke boiled into the air. The girl with Chokole swung back on her mare. Josh stood quietly at the edge of their firepit with no expression on his face. As the ponies calmed, Josh turned to Augustine.

"Tell the chief I just brewed up some real powerful magic so his people could win a war with their enemies," Josh said, and now his voice was hard, like a growl. "You can say he won't have no trouble winnin' his fight if he'll leave me alone to run my lines this winter. But I also want you to say that if he don't keep his word, them spirits will be angry as hell. Tell him all of what I said, Father." Josh's face turned mean. "An' tell him if he don't listen, I'm liable to use my magic against him. Be real damn sure you tell him that!"

"It might not be advisable to threaten him," Augustine said in a voice so small Fargo barely heard it.

Josh turned his malevolent stare on the priest. "You say it anyway," he warned.

Augustine swallowed and began a careful translation, pausing every now and then to think of a word. As he spoke, Fargo noticed how a subtle change had come to the chief's face, not altogether a look of fear, but perhaps the beginning of it.

Bull Bear held his pony in check while the priest finished delivering his message. Then he made a sign, a closed fist over his heart, before he turned his pony back up the ravine and rode away with his warriors and the women.

Once, just as Chokole was about to ride out of sight into the trees she looked over her shoulder. Fargo couldn't be sure, but it looked like she flashed him a trace of a smile before she disappeared into deep forest shadows.

18

"What do you make of it, Skye?" Josh asked, the silhouettes of Bull Bear's band vanishing in the ravine, melting into dark places away from the sun where the oaks thickened.

Fargo thought a moment. "He was damn sure surprised by the gunpowder . . ."

Augustine cast them both a worried look. "If things do not go well in their battles with the Nah-taih they will come back. I had hoped Father Olivares and I could begin our trek up the creek to our mission. However, with an Indian war beginning in this region I wonder if it would be wise to leave your protection at the moment."

Olivares sleeved sweat from his brow, still watching the ravine as if he expected the Apaches to return. "If Mr. Fargo and Mr. Brooks are in agreement, Father, I wish we could stay here with them until matters between tribes are settled. I am neither a brave man nor a coward, but I am quite sure these people would show us no mercy if they find us there. As you know, they still blamed the order for their disease."

"You're welcome to stay with Josh," Fargo said, returning his guns to a pile of packs in a corner of the lean-to, convinced that for now the trouble had passed. "You're earnin' your keep by helpin' us with this shelter an' it's a help to have Father Augustine here to tell us what they're sayin' when they show up."

"We'll be most grateful," Olivares said with obvious relief. "And I assure you we will do anything we can to assist you."

"Then it's decided," Josh remarked, walking to the cart for more bundles of cut limbs to add to the roof. "We can begin mixin' mud to sod this roof by tomorrow. Takes a while for it to dry an' we'll need to cut some tall grass to bind it together on this framework."

"I'll gladly cut whatever grass is necessary," Olivares continued. "And if you'll show me how to mix the mud required, I'll prepare it. We have clay pots the Apaches gave us and we can use the cart to ferry water from the river. It sounds very similar to mixing adobe for brick in San Antonio . . ."

"No caliche 'round here," Josh observed. "We'll have to make do with this river clay an' hope it works like it's supposed to."

Fargo hoisted an armload of branches to the framework, where he began tying it down. "Sure was glad to know that girl wasn't one of them who got her head cut off. Too bad she don't speak no more English than she does."

Augustine spoke, wrinkling his brow in memory. "She understands more than she speaks, Mr. Fargo. Actually, she learned very rapidly."

"I was sorta wonderin' why she was with the chief just now," he added. "Maybe she's one of his wives—you said some of 'em had more'n one."

As Augustine unloaded more limbs from the cart he said, "If memory serves me well she is the daughter of Bull Bear's brother, a man who was killed several years ago. It is Apache custom for other members of a family to raise children when a parent dies. She was a very good student of our language and I was so hopeful she would become an important connection between us and her tribe in the introduction of Christianity. Alas, there wasn't time before the smallpox was introduced."

Josh was still a little nervous over the arrival of Bull Bear. "I ain't all that convinced we've seen the last of them. A puff of gunsmoke won't be enough to help 'em win a war with them Comanches. I still say we oughta stay out of it if we can."

"That's what we're doin' now, Josh. Gettin' ready for cold weather so this lean-to will keep you from freezin' to death, cut a store of firewood an' such. Pretty soon we'll start hunting up some game so we can smoke deer an' turkey and fish. I'll take some smoked turkey with me when I head back south. Then you can begin scoutin' creeks for beaver dams so you know where the best beaver trappin' will be. If those Indians fight their war someplace else, you shouldn't be caught in the middle."

Augustine piled more branches near the roof frame. "There is one more thing to consider, Mr. Fargo. If the smallpox gets any worse, if it continues to spread, Bull Bear will be back asking for your assistance again." The priest frowned. "I'm sure you've considered another possibility as well. He may find a way to blame Mr. Brooks for its spread as he first blamed us for it when his people began to die. Let us hope and pray the quarantine works."

"As much as it pains me to say it, Father, the truth is, that ain't my problem. Josh and I had an agreement coming into this that I would help him get started, and then be on my way. Ain't that right, Josh?"

Josh nodded his head. "And I appreciate it. Hell, I knew from day one that this wasn't going to be easy. Of course, I didn't think I'd be using any 'magical powers' just to trap some furs, and I sure as hell never figured on being caught in no Indian war, but it's still the best chance I got to live the good life."

"But Mr. Fargo," Augustine started, "surely with all your knowledge you can help us bring civilization to these savages."

"If you feel yours is a mission worth fighting for, and it's not hurtin' no one," Fargo addressed the two priests again, "then I wish you both the best of luck with it. This ain't no game out here, and it ain't no great pioneer story waiting to be told back East, either. Men out here die unrecognized every day. If you're taking it on, you're taking it on all the way, and the only shot you've got at survival is to make the life you're leading out here your own." Fargo paused long enough to give Josh a look before continuing. "My life is one that's always on the move, and while you're trying to spread your word and he's making to catch a fortune, I'm just looking to move on. Along with what you've paid me here, those ponies I got lined up should get me enough to keep going through the next two seasons. Come winter, that's a lifesaver. If I stay here any longer, I'm all but giving up on getting through the rough months in one piece." He cast a long look across the three of them to make sure they understood that he wasn't abandoning them, then turned around and prepared to break down his camp.

19

After he'd gathered his provisions into a pack, Skye said his good-byes to Josh and the priests. Josh almost broke his ribs, giving him a giant bear hug by way of thanks for leading him to the beavers he'd been searching for.

"You take care, now, you hear?" Josh said, his eyes showing his worry about Skye traveling down the river alone.

"I'll be sure an' watch my back, Josh. You try and stay outta trouble up here. The Indian wars are nothin' to mess around with."

"Believe it, pardner," Josh said. "All I want to do is get my beavers an' make my fortune. The 'Pache can take care of theyselves."

Skye turned to the priests and held out his hand to Father Olivares. "Father, don't you worry none about your courage. I don't know many men who would've undertaken a journey alone such as you did to come up here and help Father Augustine."

Olivares ducked his head for a moment. "Thank you, my friend," he said.

"God go with you, my son," Augustine said, putting his hand on Skye's shoulder.

He shouldered his pack and walked off into the

woods, following the banks of the river toward the Indian camp downstream.

Upon his arrival, Mangas came out of his hut and greeted Skye with all the deference of a major medicine man, which he believed him to be.

Skye pulled a large iron knife from his pack and a handful of shiny red and orange beads. "Chief, I have important business to do at the mouth of the river. I'll trade these to you for a pony that'll get me there."

Skye motioned and pointed to try and get his point across. Mangas understood and nodded once, inclining his head toward a string of pinto ponies grazing in a nearby field of grass.

Skye threw a blanket over the withers of the largest of the ponies and fastened a rein to his mouth, then vaulted up on his back.

He waved at the Indians who stood watching him and turned the pony's head downstream.

It was nearing dusk when he approached the area of Bull Bear's camp. He was thinking about Chokole and trying to decide if he should drop by and say goodbye to her when he heard voices over near the river. It sounded like the laughter of girls, so he decided to take a look. He eased off the pony and made his way through the thick undergrowth, making as little noise as he could until he got near the river.

He eased some branches aside and peered out. There were seven young Indian girls swimming and frolicking in the cool waters of the stream. They were all naked, their breasts bouncing and jiggling as they splashed water at each other and laughed.

Looking at their thin, supple bodies and the way

the afternoon sun glinted and sparkled off them, he felt his groin grow heavy and begin to stiffen.

He rubbed himself, trying to decide what to do, when he noticed Chokole sitting on a rock near the river's edge, her feet dangling in the water. She was dressed in her deerskin clothes and was evidently keeping watch on the younger girls as they played.

Skye stepped partway out of the bush he was hiding behind so she could see him. He gave a small wave of his hand to get her attention.

She noticed the movement and looked over at him, at first startled, then her lips turned up in a small smile. She put a finger to her lips and motioned him back into cover.

After he was hidden again, she called sharply to the other girls, saying something in her tongue Skye didn't understand. The girls all looked disappointed, but they slowly climbed out of the water and began to put their dresses on, looking over their shoulders at Chokole with wondering glances.

Another few words and they filed off through the woods, leaving Chokole alone on the riverbank. She leaned back on her hands, making her breasts push out against the deerskin in a way that made Skye's member throb with anticipation.

He stepped to the edge of the river across from Chokole, noticing how her eyes drifted down to the large bulge in his pants.

"I'm on my way down south, Chokole," Skye said. "It'll be a while 'fore I can get back up this way."

She cocked her head, her eyes still on his groin. "You look dirty to me, Skye. Maybe you are in need of washing?"

Skye grinned and shucked his clothes off faster than

it takes to tell it. He waded into the frigid water, wincing as he felt his erection shrivel from the cold.

Chokole stood and unfastened her dress, letting it fall to the ground at her feet. Her nipples were erect, standing out from her full heavy breasts as she stepped into the water on her side and slowly swam toward him.

She glided through the water until she was in front of him, then swung around to float on her back, letting her legs wrap themselves around his hips.

As her warm pubic hair pushed against him, he responded in spite of the cold, growing thick and heavy with desire. "Your English seems better," he smiled.

Her eyes got big as she felt his member pressing against her mound and let her hands drift under water until they circled him. "I practice just in case you came back for . . . a visit," a mischievous grin spread across her face.

As he palmed her breasts, pinching and rubbing her nipples, she leaned her head back and groaned. "I had forgotten how big you are," she whispered, her eyes closed as he played with her breasts.

He dropped his right hand and put it over her pubic hair, probing with his finger until he found her soft wetness. As he rubbed her button, he rasped harshly, "I ain't forgotten nothing about you, Chokole. I remember every part."

With a groan deep in her throat, she pushed his hand aside and fitted the head of his member against her, pulling and tightening her legs until he was thrust deep inside her.

"Oh . . . oh, Skye . . ." she said as he was thrust with his hips, impaling her.

She wrapped her arms around his neck and pressed

her breasts to his chest, opening her mouth and placing it tight against his as she began to thrust with her hips, back and forth.

Skye grabbed her buttocks, pulling her against him, moving with her as fast as he could in the water, probing her mouth with his tongue and feeling himself grow even harder as she sucked on it.

She screamed into his mouth as she came, moments before he felt himself explode inside her, flooding her and causing her to quiver as she came again and again, jerking her hips, her buttocks as tight as rocks in his hands.

Later, they lay naked, wrapped in each other's arms on a bed of pine needles she'd brushed into a pile. Her cheeks were still rosy with desire and her breasts were pressed against his chest as she nibbled his ear.

His hand moved over her ripe hips, and he felt himself become hard again. He pushed her over onto her back and moved slowly down her body until his face was brushing her pubic hair. The scent of her desire was strong in his nostrils as he buried his face against her, probing her wetness with his tongue. As he moved his tongue and lips against her, she began to push against him, moaning deep in her throat.

"What are you doing . . . oh . . ."

Skye licked and sucked until she was in a frenzy.

As she became more excited, he reached up and pushed her head toward his throbbing member. Her eyes grew wide when she realized what he wanted her to do, but she didn't hesitate.

Grabbing him with both hands, she lowered her head and took him between her lips, sighing as he continued to pleasure her with his mouth.

He exploded at the same time as she went rigid in the throes of her own orgasm, bucking and moaning as she took his entire length into her mouth while he came and came.

After they were dressed, she walked with him back to the edge of the river.

"Don't worry, Chokole, I will return," Skye said.

She gave him a strange look, then looked back toward her village. "I hope I will be here to see you again, Skye."

"What do you mean by that?" he asked

"At the next sun, we go to fight the Comanches. Chief Bull Bear says it will be a dangerous war, as many of our braves are becoming sick with fever and will not be able to fight."

Damn, Skye thought. The smallpox was spreading to these Indians, too.

"But couldn't you wait until the braves are better?" he asked.

"I am afraid the Comanches will not wait, Skye. Even now they are putting on war paint and beginning their songs of death for us."

Skye made a decision. As much as it pained him, his ponies would just have to wait. Both the priests and Josh had chosen the hardships they now faced. These people had been fighting their own wars long before he had come along, but this was different. The Comanches were ruthless, and smallpox was too much of an obstacle for any army to overcome. Besides, what if there was some truth to their thinking? What if the westward travel of so many white folk had somehow caused the sickness that now threatened the very existence of tribes like this? It was not his problem, but he couldn't abandon these people to a war they couldn't win. The odds were tipped heavily against them, and the Trailsman knew that only the smoke from his Henry would be enough to level the playing field.

20

Skye told Chokole to take him to Bull Bear, for he had decided to use his "magic" to aid the Apaches in their upcoming fight against the Comanches. Chokole jumped up and threw her arms around him, telling him it was just what she hoped he'd do.

He gently untangled her arms, wishing he had time for more fun in the pine needles, and pushed her away with a wry smile.

Later, facing Bull Bear and some of his braves who weren't too sick to stand and watch, Skye spoke to him through Chokole.

"Chief, I will use my magic to help you defeat the Comanches, but for my magic to work, we must plan together the best way to defeat the enemy," Skye said, watching his face as Chokole translated.

Bull Bear idly reached over as she spoke and brushed some pine needles from her dark hair, giving Skye a look that made the hair on the back of his neck stand up.

When she finished speaking, the chief nodded once, briefly, and waited for Skye to continue.

"While I know there are no fighters on earth as brave as the mighty Apache," Skye continued, "the

Comanches do have one advantage. They are masters of war on horseback. No one can match them in face-to-face combat while mounted on ponies."

The chief scowled at this but nodded for Skye to go on.

"Therefore, it is my suggestion that when they attack, we keep a small force of braves in front of them and have the braves turn and run, causing the Comanches to follow them."

Bull Bear's scowl deepened, but he kept his lips pressed tight as Skye hurriedly went on speaking.

He turned and pointed back down the trail away from the village, which led to a deep ravine, cut deep in the limestone rocks of the region where ancient floods of the river had scoured deep crevices and winding canyons in the dirt.

"If we can make the Comanches follow our small group of braves down that trail, while we have the remainder of your braves stationed on the cliffs above, hidden among the trees and bushes, we will have them trapped in a small, narrow valley where their horses won't be an advantage. I will be waiting at the head of the valley with my thundersticks to stop them in their advance. When they stop, your braves can come out of hiding on the cliffs above them and they will be easy targets for your bows and arrows and your braves will be too high for their weapons to reach."

Skye waited while Chokole stumbled through a rough translation of his plan. He knew that unless the chief accepted, his people would stand no chance against the superior forces of the Comanches, perhaps the best horseback warriors in history.

After Chokole finished, the chief turned and spoke to an older man dressed in the traditional garb of a medicine man. Skye figured him to be one of the elders Bull Bear relied on for advice in times of trouble.

After much gesturing and pointing and what seemed to be some arguing among the two men, the chief turned back to Skye and nodded, speaking a few phrases in his language.

Chokole grabbed Skye's arm, her lips turned up in a small smile. "Chief Bull Bear agrees with your plan, though he hopes the war gods will not think the Apache cowardly for running from battle."

Skye grinned. "Tell the chief his braves will not be running from battle, just running to do battle at a more advantageous position," he said.

The chief gave his first slight smile when Chokole translated this last piece of advice. Then he whirled away to give orders to his braves to carry out Skye's instructions and to get in position atop the valley walls.

Skye spent a lonely night in a small tent by himself, wishing Chokole would find some way to visit him as he lay covered with thick buffalo robes and blankets. But the older women of the village set up station outside his tent, probably to keep just such a thing from occurring.

The Comanches attacked just after dawn the next morning. When they were met with the token force of six braves, facing more than sixty Comanches, they didn't hesitate to follow the Apache braves as they whirled their horses around and galloped down the trail leading into the deep ravine surrounded on all sides by steep cliffs and walls of limestone.

Skye had positioned himself at the head of the valley in a small group of boulders. He had both pistols on the rock in front of him, along with all his fixings of gunpowder, balls, wads, and nipple covers arrayed in front of him. His Henry rifle was lying across the boulder in front of him and he leaned behind it, sighting along the barrel up the trail as the quick-paced braves approached, followed a hundred yards back by a hoard of yelling, screaming Comanches.

Skye slowly eared back the hammer of the Henry and sighted on a large buck leading the charge. He had a huge barrel chest surrounded by heavy muscles and was carrying a bow almost as long as he was tall with an arrow notched in the rawhide string. Just as the warrior pulled the string back and took aim, Skye slowly increased pressure on the trigger until the big rifle exploded, sending a foot of flame out of the barrel and kicking back against his shoulder.

The brave clutched his chest as a hole appeared between his nipples, knocking him backward onto the rump of his pony to pinwheel in a somersault beneath the hooves of those following him, dead before he hit the ground.

Without waiting to see what effect his "thunder-stick" had on the others, Skye jacked another shell into the chamber and fired as rapidly as he could, not bothering to take aim at specific targets but firing into the milling crowd of Indians as they jerked their ponies to a halt.

Several more braves hit the dirt, dead or severely wounded before Skye ran out of ammunition in his Henry. He threw the rifle to the ground, reached for his Colt and stepped out from behind his boulder cover. He screamed at the top of his lungs and began to fire as he walked slowly toward the terrified Indians.

As he advanced, Bull Bear's braves on the cliffs overlooking the valley appeared from their cover and began to rain arrows and spears down on the hapless Comanches, who were so disorganized by the sight and sound of Skye's gun they had yet to return to the attack.

One by one the Comanche braves were knocked from their mounts by arrows and spears. Some tried to fire upward with their own bows, but the arrows fell far short of the top of the cliffs and no Apaches were injured.

Two of the Comanches screwed up their courage enough to charge their mounts toward Skye, holding lances in front of them with the intention of running him through.

He knocked one from his horse with his last bullet, then dropped the Colt and pulled the Arkansas toothpick from his boot, vowing to go down fighting, though he knew he had little chance against a lance wielded from horseback.

He crouched, holding the blade in front of him, waiting for the end.

Suddenly, the braves who'd ridden past earlier, leading the Comanches into the trap, galloped by Skye, heading into the melee with whoops and hollers and screams as they went on the attack against the disorganized Comanches.

The brave riding toward Skye was knocked from his pony, three arrows in his chest and stomach as the Apaches rode by.

By noon, the battle was over. Four Comanche braves managed to get their ponies turned around and headed back out of the valley the way they'd come.

Over fifty of their comrades lay dead or wounded on the ground as the Apaches swarmed down the cliffs like angry ants to run among them, counting coup and taking scalps and slitting throats of the men lying on the ground.

Skye, no stranger to combat, felt the bile rise in his throat at the sight of such savagery and turned and walked back to pick up his weapons and make his way back to the village on foot, turning his head from the slaughter as he passed.

Over many campfires that night, braves danced and sang of their victory over their hated enemy, and more than one sang of the strong magic of Skye Fargo, the man called Trailsman.

Bull Bear sat by a fire in front of his tent with Skye and Chokole, along with three of his wives and four of his children.

As he spoke, Chokole translated.

"Chief Bull Bear says you have given us a great victory today. It will be many moons before the Comanches grow the courage to face us in battle again. He asks if there is anything you desire from him to honor what you have done today."

"I would first trade my pony for a canoe to take me downriver if he feels this is fair. I can make much better time on the river than on horseback."

After she gave this message to the chief and he nodded, Skye continued. "Ask him if it is possible, this last night among your people, for you to stay with me in my tent. You can tell the chief that I want to teach you some of the secrets of my magic so that you may impart them to your people after I leave."

Chokole smiled. "The chief is no fool, Skye. After

all, he is a man as well as a chief of my people. He will know why you want me to share your blanket."

Skye shrugged. "Then, if he is a man first and a chief second, he will understand. Ask him, Chokole, if it will not shame you among your people to do this openly."

She shook her head. "To lie with a man with such strong medicine is no dishonor, Skye. I will ask."

When she finished talking, the chief turned his eyes on Skye and nodded, the corners of his mouth turning up in a very small smile, as if he knew what desire Chokole could evoke in a man.

Bull Bear got to his feet and walked away, chanting and singing as he joined his braves in their victory dance around the fires.

Skye thought he detected envy in the eyes of Bull Bear's wives as they stared at her and him before following their man toward the fires.

Skye was finishing the last of a bowl of buffalo stew, sopping up the juice with a type of cornbread some older women of the tribe had brought to him when Chokole appeared in the doorway to his tent.

She slipped inside and stood before him, dressed in a beaded deerskin dress that was much more ornate than the one she usually wore. Her hair was braided and wild flowers were entwined in the dark tresses, accentuating the almost blue-black color of her hair.

He felt a familiar stirring in his groin as she untied the fastening and let the dress fall to the floor. She stood over him, her breasts heaving with desire as she stared down at him lying among the buffalo skins on the dirt floor of his tent.

He reached up, letting his hand caress her pubic hair, already moist with her longing.

"Come here," he said in a husky voice.

Without hesitation, she bent and tugged and pulled at his shirt and pants until he was naked as she was, then she pushed him onto his back and straddled him, letting his member slide into her until their pubic bones touched.

She sighed and threw her head back in ecstasy as he began to move under her.

Later, as they lay in each other's arms, she rose up on one elbow and stared into his eyes, hooded with the sleepiness that comes from satisfaction.

"Skye, are you ready for sleep?" she asked, shyly.

He glanced at her, wondering what she had on her mind.

"Not especially. Why?"

She pulled the hairy buffalo robe off his chest and ran her hands down his flat stomach. "Because, if you are not too tired, I would like to try once again what we did at the river yesterday. I long for the taste of your . . . lance once again and to feel your lips on my . . ."

She didn't get to finish before Skye had rolled over to lie next to her, his face buried in her pubic hair as she grabbed his member, licking her lips, her eyes wide with delight at this newfound pleasure.

21

The next morning, just before dawn, Skye gently untangled Chokole's arms from around his neck and slipped out of the buffalo blankets. He got dressed, then bent and kissed her gently on the lips before slipping out of the tent's doorway.

He found his pack lying next to a single-man canoe on the banks of the river. He glanced back over his shoulder. Only the older women of the village were stirring, starting their cooking fires for the upcoming breakfast. The men were still all asleep in their tents, exhausted from the celebration that had gone on until well past midnight the night before.

The women gave him sly glances, but wouldn't meet his eyes when he looked. He figured they couldn't wait to talk to Chokole to see just how the white-eyes fared when compared with the men who shared their blankets.

With a wry smile, he climbed into the canoe and pushed out into the fast-flowing water.

As he let the force of the water move him, only paddling occasionally to keep the canoe in the middle of the current, he glanced at the surrounding red-stone cliffs that rose on either side of the river, thinking back on how the land had helped him defeat the Comanches. Sometimes it was just the way of the land, depositing fortunes for some and hardships for others. The Comanches failed to show the land its proper respect. All they knew was that they wanted more of it, but unfortunately for them, they forgot to listen and pay attention to what it wanted from them. Sometimes it wants you to stay, sometimes to go, and sometimes if you're lucky, it wants you to take a look between the shrubs and trees and find swimming treasures that giggle with delight. All it wanted from the Comanches was for them to look up before stumbling into a trap, but in the end, maybe it was too pleased that he and the Apache had taken advantage of its fine features to bother telling them that.

As for himself, all Skye Fargo wanted was to get away from the river and back to the land so he could return to the endless trail once again. There was plenty out there still to see, and a temperamental landscape of opportunities to be had, but the only way to them was to keep moving. The Trailsman aimed to do just that.

LOOKING FORWARD!
The following is the opening section from the next novel in the exciting *Trailsman* series from Signet:

THE TRAILSMAN #240
FRISCO FILLY

San Francisco, California 1859—
All the world's a stage—and some of the players are more deadly than others.

Skye Fargo rode with renewed energy. It had been a long month since he had left Kansas City behind in a dust cloud of outlaws and Indians. The raging prairie fire that had forced him to detour far to the south into Texas only made things worse. But never in that month had he considered not delivering the package wrapped in oilcloth and stuffed into his saddlebags. Arthur Nance had been a good friend, and Fargo had promised him on his dying bed that the bundle in question would be placed in the hands of his brother, Clay.

Keeping his promise proved to be a difficult task as trouble continued to pop up around every bend. After Texas he found himself in a dismal New Mexico town, run by an outlaw gang. The marshal had been even more crooked than the road agents. To make matters worse, the gang leader had taken a fancy to Fargo's Ovaro. When Fargo caught him trying to make his fancy a reality, he had no choice but to educate the man in proper manners. After leaving him dead on the ground, a bullet in his thieving heart. Fargo had hightailed it out of New Mexico with seven bloodthirsty bandits on his trail. He had reached the Rockies, and eluding them then had been easy. He knew the ways of the mountains. They had not.

He wasn't called the Trailsman for nothing.

All that difficulty lay behind him now. He felt the stiff sea breeze from the Pacific Ocean in his face alternate with the cold wind gusting off the Sierra Nevadas at his back. It had been some time since he had seen the Golden Gate, and he reckoned as to how he wouldn't mind spending a spell there again.

He craned his neck around and looked at the soaring, snow-capped Sierras. That was where he would head. Find Clay Nance, give him his inheritance, spend some time in San Francisco until he got his fill of civilization and then head back into the mountains where he belonged. No matter how much time he spent on the prairie or desert, along the coast or traveling waterways, Fargo loved the mountains best.

Fargo sucked in another deep breath of salt air, then paused. On the faint breeze blowing inland he caught a small sound, a tiny noise another man might have missed. His keen ears picked out the clamor and deciphered its meaning. Fargo reached down and made sure his Colt rested easy in its holster. There was trouble ahead.

The horse responded with a burst of speed that took them to the top of a hill where he could look down on the winding dirt road snaking off toward Oakland. His sharp lake-blue eyes found the source of the noise immediately. A stagecoach rattled along the road almost a mile off pursued by four road agents.

Fargo had had his fill of outlaws since leaving Kansas City, but he was not the man to abandon the driver and any passengers to their fate. It struck him as odd that there was not a shotgun guard alongside the driver, but as he galloped down the road in pursuit he saw the reason.

Fargo yanked back on the reins causing the Ovaro to dig in and skid to a halt. He hit the dirt running and knelt beside the man in the ditch alongside the road. The guard had been ventilated good. Rather than count the bullets that had pierced the man's chest, Fargo let him flop back down lifelessly. He didn't have time to give the man a proper burial. That had to come later.

Snatching up the man's shotgun a few yards away, Fargo checked the chambers. Both had been fired. A quick search of the guard's pockets turned up a box of shells. Fargo stuffed as many shells as he could into his own pockets, loaded the shotgun, then whistled. The Ovaro trotted over so he could mount and chase down the road agents.

Fargo put his heels to the Ovaro's flanks, and the

tired horse responded as if rested. The powerful stallion ran like the wind, and Fargo slowly narrowed the distance between him and the outlaws still throwing lead at the stage in an effort to force the driver to stop.

After what had happened to his shotgun messenger, the driver wasn't about to surrender easily. He had to think the outlaws meant to kill everyone on the stage.

For all Fargo knew, there might be a large shipment of gold aboard that the driver was willing to protect all the way to his grave.

The Ovaro strained, and its flanks became flecked with foam but the distance between the lagging outlaw and Fargo narrowed. It took several minutes before Fargo got close enough to be effective.

"Who're you?" the outlaw shouted, twisting around so he could fire his six-shooter at Fargo. Fargo cut loose with both barrels of the shotgun. The outlaw lifted in the saddle, his arms flailed and he clawed at the air. Then he hit the ground, as dead as the guard whose weapon Fargo used so effectively.

Knees gripping the sides of his steady horse, Fargo used both hands to knock open the chamber and put in two more shells. He snapped the shotgun receiver closed and bent low to reduce the target area the remaining three road agents had.

Only one noticed what had happened. He let out a yell to warn the other two, but they either were too intent on the stage to slow or didn't hear him. The outlaw began throwing lead in Fargo's direction. Every shot went wild. Fargo could have fired the shotgun in reply but chose to get closer. Still bent low, he lifted the shotgun and fired just as a chunk of his broad-brimmed hat was blown away by the outlaw's only well-aimed bullet.

Recoiling and off balance as he fired the shotgun, Fargo lost his grip on the weapon. It went flying, but so did the road agent. The man landed hard, cursing a blue streak. Fargo's buckshot had caught him in the arm, leaving it bloody and useless.

Fargo galloped past the robber and closed the distance with the remaining pair. His stallion, powerful as it was, began to flag under the strain of galloping so long and for so far. Whatever happened, it had to happen fast.

Fargo rode closer to the masked man on the side away from the driver. He could have fired shot after shot from his Colt but knew better. To hit anything—or anyone—from the back of a galloping horse took more luck than skill. Gripping his lariat, Fargo pulled the rope loose and swung it like a whip. There was no time and no need to lasso the outlaw. The rough hemp caught the rider across the face and knocked him off balance. As he struggled to maintain his mount, Fargo lashed out again. This time the rope landed with a loud "thwack" across the rump of the other horse. The mare lurched and then bucked, pitching the outlaw into the dirt. He hit the ground, rolled and then lay still.

He might have broken his neck or just been knocked out. That was something to check later. The fourth and remaining road agent fired with single-minded determination as he tried to force the coach driver to stop. Fargo let out a warning cry when he saw the rider draw a second six-gun and fire both of them.

The driver gasped, threw up his hands and then fell forward, tumbling behind the flashing hooves of his team. A red spray floated back, marking the driver's unpleasant death. But Fargo knew there would be more deaths unless he stopped the runaway team. Inside the coach he saw no fewer than three passengers and possibly a fourth, hunkered down in the center of the coach between the seats.

"The driver's dead," he shouted at a passenger who stuck his head out. The sudden wind sent the man's bowler spinning through the air. "Can you get up to the driver's box and stop the team?"

Fargo answered his own question when he saw the frightened look on the man's pasty face. Fear held the man locked in place.

"It's mine!" came the angry cry from the other side of the coach. "I'm the one robbing this here stage!" The outlaw fired through the compartment at Fargo. Two bullets blasted splinters off the doors. The other slugs sailed through harmlessly because everyone inside the coach now cowered down on the floor.

Fargo knew better than to argue. He found himself faced with a deadly dilemma. If he jumped to the stage to stop the thundering team, he would be shot down as the driver and guard had been. But shooting it out with the outlaw from horseback meant the stage and all its passengers would be in peril.

Gathering his feet under him, Fargo trusted instinct, leapt and caught the rear canvas over the passengers' luggage. He clawed the tough cloth and pulled himself to the top of the coach where he flopped belly down.

The outlaw still paced the coach—until he saw Fargo. He realized Fargo could shoot him out of the saddle unless he slackened. Reluctantly he slowed and let the out-of-control team pull the stagecoach out of six-gun range. The last Fargo heard of the man was a steady stream of curses at losing such rich plunder.

Struggling to pull himself forward, Fargo swung his feet around and dropped into the driver's box. He saw that the driver had gripped the reins too tightly and had carried them with him as he fell. From inside the coach Fargo heard shouting. The stagecoach rattled and rocked too perilously for them to jump with any expectation of doing it safely. Still, to risk death while trying to jump clear offered them at least half a chance at survival. Waiting for the runaway horses to finally succeed in toppling the stage gave them no hope at all.

Fargo braced himself and used both feet to push against the brake. The loud screech of wood being pressed into the front wheel heartened him—until the handle broke off. Fargo almost plunged forward in the same way the driver had.

"Stop us! Please!" came the plaintive cry. "O merciful Hecate, goddess of the crossroads, where is thy charity for such troubled pilgrims as we?"

Fargo glanced back and thought he was seeing things. A woman about as lovely as anything he had seen in a month of Sundays sat outlined in the front window of the passenger compartment, a china white hand pressed down into her ample bosom as she struck a pose and continued reciting words that belonged to another time and place.

Fargo scrambled about and righted himself. The brake handle had snapped near the wood pad and eliminated any chance of slowing the runaway team. Without thinking, he slipped out of the box and gingerly stepped onto the tongue of the yoke holding the back two horses. The quickest way of stopping the team was to make his way to the front pair and grab the bits of bridle remaining. That was also the surest way to slip and die.

His powerful hands clutched at the fragments of leather remaining in the tack. He got a grip on one intact rein and pulled as hard as he could. The horse to his left began to turn away from the others, causing them to break stride and slow. Muscles tense and tendons at the point of breaking, Fargo pulled with all his might to turn the four twelve-hundred-pound horses.

Just when he thought he could not hold on for another second, the lead horses slowed of their own accord and soon came to a halt. Fargo was reluctant to let his tiny piece of bridle fall loose, fearing the horses might bolt and run again. He edged forward, walking on the yokes now until he got to the front pair of horses. He gentled them for a minute, then walked back to the passenger compartment.

"Are you folks all right?" he asked, opening the bullet-riddled door.

The woman who had been spouting the strange words looked up, stricken. Her pale gray eyes brimmed with tears. She held up bloodstained hands, looked at them, then looked back at the man sprawled on the floor.

" 'All tragedies are finished by a death,' " she said softly.

"What?" Fargo knew the man was dead but couldn't fathom what the woman meant.

"Byron," she said.

"Was Byron your husband?" Fargo asked sympathetically.

"He's not Byron. This is my manager, Randolph Setts."

"But you called him Byron." Fargo didn't understand, but looking at the woman was good enough to erase some of the exasperation he felt. She had ash-blonde hair that had once been tastefully coiffed, high cheekbones and a patrician look that appealed greatly to him. As she half-turned, he saw the swell of her ample breasts and even a hint of bare flesh through a tear in her blouse. She seemed oblivious to the effect she had on him.

"I was quoting Byron. 'All tragedies are finished by a death, All comedies are ended by a marriage; The future states of both are left to faith.' "

Fargo got lost in her words and stared for another moment before shaking himself free of the spell she wove.

"We've got to get moving. I only stopped three of the robbers. There was a fourth, and he seemed mighty determined to rob your stage."

"At the depot where we boarded, I heard them talking about a gold shipment," she said dismissively. "I thought nothing of it."

"You should have, you stupid whore," shouted the man who had lost his bowler. "You could have told me, and I'd have known to take another stage!"

"Apologize." Fargo said without turning.

"What did you say?"

"Apologize to the lady." Fargo turned and loomed above the man like an avenging angel ready to swoop down. His hand rested on the butt of his Colt and every muscle was like a coiled spring, ready to unleash deadly energy. The man saw the look in Fargo's ice-blue eyes and swallowed hard.